Oh, NANTUCKET

PETER M. BROWNE

Peter M. Browne/Oh, Nantucket
Printed in the United States of America
petermbrowne.com - info@petermbrowne.com

Front Cover Satellite Image:
Ian Grasshoff
Smart mAPPS Consulting

Oh, Nantucket/ Peter M. Browne. -- 1st ed.

ISBN 978-1-7360217-0-5 Print Edition

ISBN 978-1-7360217-1-2 Ebook Edition

OH, NANTUCKET

When summer breezes blow,
They bring back memories of long ago.
When days were long and filled with joy,
When life was new,
You were a boy.

The island sang its song to you,
It promised things that could come true.

You danced and played with summer fun,
Not heeding what was yet to come.

So, as the days grow shorter now,
You look upon with furrowed brow.

What could have been,
But now you feel the winter wind.

To all my Cape Verdean brothers and sisters with the greatest love and affection and in memory of our parents and grandparents for their sacrifices

Dios ba ku nhos

PREFACE

....

THIS TALE CONCERNS A PLACE, A TIME, AND THE struggles inflicted upon a culture by deliberate social dissonance. The story is neither fact nor fiction but rather originates from the eye of the beholder, the place where reality resides.

PROLOGUE

··

DANIEL MONTEIRO WAS IN HIS 85TH SUMMER. FOR most of his life, his world had been confined to a strip of land 12 miles long and three miles wide, 30 miles at sea off the coast of Massachusetts.

For the last ten years his world had been reduced further to a 14 by 12 room at Our Island Home, a 45-bed nursing home owned by the Town of Nantucket. Most of the rooms were semi-private, each with a large window, some with a view of the creeks and Nantucket Harbor. Daniel had one of the few private rooms because of his cantankerous nature. His roommates found him less than collegial. His room was on the street side of the building, providing a view of the road, the building's entrance and nothing else.

Most days Daniel sat by the window that overlooked the roadway in his wheelchair staring out into the nothingness that was his life. Inside, the walls were barren. There was a double bed, a dresser, one nightstand. A small lamp sat on the nightstand with a plain heat-stained shade. The bedspread's nautical pattern was extremely faded, the result of too many washings. A black and white photo of a young girl no more than twenty years old was displayed on the dresser.

In his younger days, he managed to venture "off-island," as the natives called the mainland. He made it as far as New Bedford once or twice, but his memory was cloudy on the details. He could not abide the fast pace and crowds of people.

Daniel stared out the window seeing nothing when his favorite nurse, Monica, a young cheery woman, called out his name.

"Mr. Monteiro, there's someone here to see you."

Daniel had not had a visitor in years. All his family and friends had predeceased him or had moved away. He turned as quickly as he could, which was pretty darned slow, to see a young lady standing in the doorway. She was tall and fairly slender, dressed in a black pantsuit and white blouse. She was light complected with dark, shoulder-length hair. She appeared to be in her early twenties.

Daniel stared at her for a while, trying to figure out who she might be and why she'd come to visit. He didn't come up with any working theories, but that wasn't surprising because his mind wasn't as sharp as it once was.

"Mr. Monteiro, my name is Anna Fortes." She gave the nurse a dismissive nod and crossed the room. "I'm with the Nantucket Historical Society. May I speak with you?"

Daniel wore a questioning look and cleared his throat as his lips formed the words. His voice felt rusty. "What's this about? Are you trying to sell me something?"

She laughed. "No, not at all. Let me explain." As she approached Daniel, she took the only chair in the room and placed it beside him. Anna sat down with both feet flat on the floor and leaned in toward Daniel. She repeated a little louder. "I'm from the Nantucket Historical Society," and she paused to see if Daniel understood her. Appearing unsure about what to say next, she asked, "How are you doing today?"

Daniel remained stoic with his jaw clenched.

Anna pressed in an effort to make a connection. She noticed the vacant look in his eyes and seemed concerned that it may have been a mistake coming here.

She tried again. "Is it okay if we talk?"

After a protracted silence, Daniel responded. "Sure. What's this about?"

Anna told him for the third time that she was with the Nantucket Historical Society. "I'd like to talk to you about your experiences growing up on Nantucket during the early 1900s and what you may have been told about the years before then, if that's okay."

Daniel turned to gaze out the window, then turned back to look at Anna. He repeated, "Sure. What's this about?" His throat felt dry and scratchy, his voice unpracticed. He didn't speak much through-out the day; there just wasn't much to talk about anymore, except for aches and pains. And Daniel was bored with talk of maladies.

Anna explained that the Historical Society had come under pressure to redo the current exposition on Cape Verdean culture. She said that the current piece had come under fire in recent years for a lack of any true content. "It's a bunch of static pictures with meaningless and inaccurate captions. I want it to tell our real sto-ry," she said.

It was true that individually and collectively the Cape Verdeans didn't appear in the historical records in any significant way.

"There's just a single webpage, which some people find offen-sive. I want to make sure our story is told in a way that recognizes our humanity," Anna said, clearly trying to impress Daniel with the importance of their meeting. "You're the last of your generation.

The history of our people on this island before you is lost to time. Help me to preserve what remains," she said, her voice rich with emotion.

Daniel wasn't quite sure what to make of this. He didn't know how to say it to Anna, so he whispered, "There's not a lot worth telling."

She registered the doubt in his eyes. "Just talk to me. Tell me about your life, what you remember, what you felt, what you experienced. You must certainly have memories worth sharing," she probed.

Daniel's eyes teared up as old memories flooded his mind. "Well, alright. If you insist." He began to tell his story.

ONE

....

I STOOD ON THE COMMERCIAL WHARF OVERLOOKING
Nantucket Harbor. I felt the warm mid-May air on my face, as the
water temperature in the harbor moderated the air close to shore.

I had just come from downtown, where clerks and shopkeep-
ers were busily performing their pre-summer ritual, removing the
island's cloak of winter, and replacing it with its summer mantle.
As boarded windows were uncovered, new coats of paint were ap-
plied, and dust and musk were removed from shuttered stores, restaurants, and shops.

It was the summer of 1942 and I was going to be 18, born on
July 3rd. As a youth, I had wished my mother could have held out
another day. Then everyone would celebrate my birthday with
fireworks. It was a childish notion, one that I increasingly relin-
quished with each passing year.

I was looking forward to this summer. I had survived winter,
and like all winters, it had been desolate, bleak, and endless. So
very wintery. Perhaps the bleaker the winter, the more vibrant the
summer, I hoped.

Summer was always an adventure. People flocked to the island from all over the world. The erstwhile empty streets bulged
with summer residents and day trippers, cars and bicycles were

7

everywhere, the harbor filled with boats and Main Street came alive with shoppers, tourists, and street vendors selling local vegetables and homemade goods.

I could hardly wait until Memorial Day when it all began.

I turned and headed for home. I had been walking around just to kill time. This would probably be my last idle day until Labor Day returned the island to its winter mode, a thought I quickly discarded.

As I approached my house, Aunt Mabel yelled, "Danny, where have you been? We've been looking all over for you! We need to get going." She was my mother's younger sister.

"I thought we were supposed to start housecleaning tomorrow," I said in my defense.

"Get in the truck," she said dismissively.

The next two weeks would be dominated by the spring-cleaning frenzy heralding the beginning of the summer season. Cape Verdeans, the unskilled labor force on the island, descended like locusts on the homes of the wealthy, cleaning windows, scrubbing floors, painting decks, raking yards, and mowing lawns. They brought with them every available member of the family, regardless of age. Each person was represented as a full-fledged working adult on the property owner's bill. This practice, inflating the workforce, was a tradition, with both sides being complicit in the scheme. It was an unspoken contract. The wealthy wanted their houses cleaned and ready for occupancy, no matter the cost. The local labor force had a limited number of opportunities to earn money and a short timeframe within which to do it—the thirteen weeks between Memorial Day and Labor Day.

"Let's get going," my aunt commanded. Aunt Mabel was the leader of our extended family of Monteiros and Vieiras. She was the businesswoman of the extended family, the one who did all the upfront work, interacting with clients, purchasing supplies, doling out work assignments, collecting payments, and handling disbursements.

We were headed to the Merriweather Mansion in Monomoy.

I climbed into the back of the truck, along with the rest of the crew, including my younger sister, three cousins, and one of my older brothers. My brother drove and my mother rode shotgun.

Of course, Aunt Mabel drove her own car, a 1934 Studebaker. She refused to be seen riding in a truck like poor folks.

It was just a 1.5-mile drive from our house on Washington Street to Monomoy, but in reality, the two properties were worlds apart.

As we approached the Merriweather Mansion at the end of a winding dirt road, it looked more like a hotel than a residence. The property was a 12-bedroom, 6,000-square-foot house on five acres, located on the waterfront, with a full view of Nantucket harbor.

When we turned off the main road, I stood up in the back of the truck to see where we were going.

"Sit down, stupid. You're going to fall out," said my younger sister Eugenia, tugging on my pantleg to get my attention.

I kicked my leg to shake her off. "Get up here and look at this," I said.

Eugenia was barely 14, but she had been housecleaning since she was ten. Eugenia remained seated. "What's to see? How rich people live? I don't care. I'm just here 'cause Mai said I have to come 'cause we need the money."

Mai is mother or mom in Kriolu, Cape Verdean Creole, a Portuguese-based creole language originating on the islands of Cape Verde off the western coast of Africa.

"I'd rather play with Clara. Her mother doesn't make her do housecleaning. How come I have to do it?"

"You know why," I said, still checking out the expansive property, imagining what it would be like to live there. "You said it yourself."

"I know but still," she said.

The truck pulled onto the crushed scallop-shell driveway with the '34 Studebaker following closely behind.

Aunt Mabel parked, jumped out of her car, and immediately barked out orders. "Get those cleaning supplies inside! Take the cans of paint around back! Girls in the kitchen. Danny, start washing the windows on the first floor."

We put in a full day of mind-numbing manual labor. Aunt Mabel prepared lunch for everyone and called us into the kitchen when it was time to eat. Lunch was brief because time was money and lunchtime wasn't recorded on her timesheet.

I cleaned windows for several hours. The colonial window panes were 12 inches tall and eight inches wide with 12 panes to a window. I lost count of the number of panes I had cleaned by the time I reached the kitchen windows. The kitchen windows were open to rid the house of the musty scent of winter.

As I approached the open windows, I could hear Aunt Mabel's voice inside the house.

"Veronica told me that her husband, Ray, has moved in with some *branka*."

A branka was a white woman in Kriolu.

"Who?" asked Mai.

"She wouldn't say, but it has to be that school teacher we've seen in his truck."

"Ava Pierce?"

"Yeah, that's the one."

"She can't be a day over 25, and he's, what, 42 or 43?"

"Yup. I've seen them more than once riding around. I guess he thinks that no one will notice what they're up to, or perhaps he just doesn't care."

"He and Veronica have been married how long?"

"At least 15 years. Their oldest kid is 12 or 13."

"No good can come of this. Where will they go? What will they do? The brankas aren't going to accept him and the Cape Verdeans certainly won't accept her. They're done on this island for sure."

"People need to learn to stick to their own kind," said Aunt Mabel.

I listened intently, carefully hidden from sight. I had learned so much about people's personal affairs by eavesdropping on my aunt's and mother's gossip sessions.

When I was younger, I used to sit in the living room listening to their conversations. When they got to the juicy parts, they would switch to Kriolu, believing I couldn't understand and I would play along. *If they only knew*, I thought, smiling to myself. Having heard enough, I decided to see how my brother was doing in the back yard.

I, too, had seen Ray Pereira around town with Ava Pierce but made nothing of it. Ray wasn't the first Cape Verdean I had seen her with. She was coupled up at a beach party in Dionis last summer with Domingo Tavares and before that, Tony Lopes. I considered her an honorary Cape Verdean because she was also good friends with Angie Silva.

She is one of the few brankas on Nantucket who's color blind. One of the open-minded brankas, I thought.

TWO

....

"MR. MONTEIRO?" ANNA FORTES CALLED OUT FROM the doorway to his room.

Daniel swiveled his wheelchair around to greet her and straightened his slumped posture. "Oh, I can hear you just fine. No need to shout, young lady."

She stood in the doorway, with her hand pressed against the doorframe, as though she were waiting for an invitation to enter his private world.

"Come on in, why don't you? I promise I won't bite," he said chuckling to himself. He was happy to discover that he still had a sense of humor. He didn't get much of a chance to use it at *Our Lost Island Home*, as he liked to call it. He would say to anyone who would listen, "Cuz anyone who comes here is never found or rescued. The door only swings one way—in."

"How are you doing today?" Anna asked with an optimistic lilt in her voice as if she expected him to have some news worth sharing.

This was her usual greeting which Daniel consistently ignored, not because he was unsociable, but because he didn't like telling lies or even half-truths. And if he had answered her question honestly, he would've said, "I'm not *doing* anything. At best I'm just being, which I know is all the rage these days—everyone is trying to be, not doing. And, trust me, this being nonsense is overrated. At worst, I'm sitting here waiting to die, to get it over with—join the rest of my family. Especially Aunt Mabel," he said sarcastically.

At the mention of Aunt Mabel, Anna perked up as if she had a question about her on the tip of her tongue. But instead she said, "I have really enjoyed our last few…" She smiled a bit awkwardly, clearly searching for the perfect word. "Talks."

Daniel grinned. He was pleased to see her and to have the opportunity to talk with someone who, on the surface, appeared to be interested in him and his stories. He hoped she wasn't just being polite. *Could a young woman like Anna really enjoy the company of an old fogie like me?*

She approached the only chair in Daniel's room and said, "May I?"

He motioned to offer her a seat. "Xinta, nha fidja," sit my child. Daniel was delighted to have the rare opportunity to speak a few words of Kriolu, with Anna. He looked up at her. "Old habits…" He had to chuckle to himself, as he heard himself speaking Kriolu and thought, *how many times had his parents uttered that very phrase? I've become my parents.*

"Mutu obrigadu," thank you, Anna responded, with a smile, completing the exchange. Their expressions conveyed that they both enjoyed their little repartee. She then pulled the chair closer to Daniel, and settled into it.

She brought in a scent from the outside world—like the most fragrant wild roses that grew all over the island. It was a nice change from the alternating stale and disinfectant odors that lurked in the rooms and hallways of Our Island Home. The scent of wild roses triggered a memory that Daniel had pushed back into the recesses of his mind.

"Where were we, last time we spoke? Ah, yes, you were telling me about opening rich people's summer homes," she said, her hands crossed in her lap.

Daniel was anxious to pick up the story, partly to share it with her and partly to transport himself back to the summer of '42, the last time he felt truly alive.

"Yes, that lasted about two weeks, from sunrise to sunset, from Monomoy to Surfside, to Polpis, and a few houses on Upper Main Street. When it was over, I was exhausted. We cleaned so many windows, I thought my arm might fall off. But as you can see, I was mistaken." With a playful grin, he waved his right arm to show it was still intact. "So, I took a few days off before looking for a summer job."

Scurrying through the kitchen toward the front door of our home, I said "Mai, I'm headed uptown. Need anything?"

"Where you going?" she asked, scrubbing the kitchen stove.

"Going to look for a job." I wanted this summer to be different. And not just where work was concerned, also in so many other aspects of my life. I secretly hoped there might be a girl out there who would notice me, but to be honest, I didn't think it was possible. I wondered if I was every bit the dork my cousin Terry thought I was.

"Can you pick up some bread and milk on your way back?"

"Sure. Anything else?"

"Yes, take this dish back to Aunt Mabel's," she said, trying to hand me a glass casserole dish.

Darn! I should've left while the going was good. Stopping at Aunt Mabel's was something I tried to avoid at all costs. I stuffed my hands in my pants pockets to signal they were out of commission. "Not now, Mai. I'll do it later." I had to be careful not to sound irritated. Disrespecting our elders was not something our generation did, unlike the kids today.

I rushed for the front door before I could be assigned any more unpleasant chores.

I had walked up Washington Street thousands of times, but each time I passed the house next door, I wondered about the family who lived there. As far as I could tell they were Merkanus di kor, which translated into Colored Americans. It was what Cape Verdeans called people of color who were not Cape Verdeans, as a means of disassociating with them. The term could be descriptive or pejorative depending on how it was used.

The next-door neighbors were very dark complected with pronounced ethnic features. An elderly man would often sit out on the front porch. We would exchange a friendly nod but we never spoke to one another. I didn't really know what to say to him.

My mother called him Boneka, which I'd assumed was his name. It wasn't until many years later that I found out that *boneka* meant doll in Kriolu. Boneka was a diminutive man, but I thought calling him a *boneka* was cruel. As it turned out, it was simply my mother's sense of humor. She had nicknames for many people that were only spoken in our house or shared with Aunt Mabel during one of their many gossip sessions. Marie Melada was another of her favorites. Marie had the same skin condition as Michael Jackson—vitiligo or blotchy two-toned skin. Marie Melada translated into dirty Mary.

As he told the story, Daniel realized that his mother might sound cruel or insensitive to Anna. "Don't get me wrong. My mother was a wonderful woman—loving, kind, generous, polite, extremely religious, but gossip was her sole source of entertainment. And making up names for people that they would never hear was, well, just part of it. She meant no harm."

The Rileys lived next to Boneka's house. With that name, I supposed they were Irish. Again, the only interaction with them was a passing nod. The rest of Washington Street, all the way to the dry cleaners on the corner, was nothing but an open field with grass as tall as me. Next was the American Legion Hall. The only time I saw the inside was when it was rented for a wedding or a funeral, there were no Cape Verdean members.

Margaret Santos lived in the house next to the Legion. It was tucked into the lot like an afterthought. Its walls were so close to the Legion, if you opened the window you could touch the bricks of the building without reaching very far.

Margaret was an odd duck. She dressed like a gypsy and conducted seances and read Tarot cards. I was in her house once and was totally freaked out. Whenever I walked past her house, I hurried for two reasons. I wanted to get past any evil juju lurking around her lot and to escape the clutches of Aunt Mabel, whose house was next door. I could never get past her place without being asked to perform a chore, run an errand, or convey a message back to my mother. Of course, the last of these wasn't a big deal and didn't require much effort. But getting roped into Aunt Mabel's universe usually meant one thing: work.

So, as I approached her home, I picked up my pace, regretting that I hadn't taken Union Street to town to avoid her place altogether. Just as I was thinking I had made this strategic error I heard her commanding voice. She must have had radar for potential targets. She wouldn't possibly have been sitting in the window watching for passersby. Or had she been?

"Danny, precious, come here a minute."

That was her famous clarion cry. *Precious, come here a minute.* You knew it was going to be *way* more than a minute. The more she sweet-talked you, the more she would ask you to do. Aunt Mabel would give you the shirt off her back but would always remind you of the shirt and use it to exact your last drop of blood as repayment.

"The Godfather had nothing on her," Daniel said, grinning.

"Sounds like it," Anna said, entranced by his story. "Your aunt sounds like a character."

"Oh, yes, indeed. If she had been alive today, she would've been a CEO of some major corporation or some kind of politician."

"Danny, precious, come here. Can you take those screens down off the windows, so I can wash them?"

There was no saying no to Aunt Mabel. First, my mother would have killed me and second, she left you no room to refuse her overtures, because she had you in her debt. Remember the "shirt" she gave you.

So, I completed the chore as quickly as possible and left without saying anything, because a conversation could remind her of another assignment that she wouldn't hesitate to give me.

From there it was smooth sailing to Main Street, except for the spaniel in the corner house, who would charge the fence and scare the crap out of you, if you didn't remember it was going to happen. It got loose once and bit me as I rode by on my bike, so I was always on the lookout.

My plan was to hit every business on Main Street and then all the side streets, until somebody hired me.

For the past few summers, I had worked in the kitchen of several restaurants and I wanted to do something else besides washing dishes. It was tedious and thankless, not to mention steamy. I hoped to find a job with more status. You'd think that wouldn't be too hard—right?

My first stop, Colson's Clothing Store, where I was immediately intercepted by a blonde clerk dressed in a nautical style, all red, white, and blue. "Can I help you?" she said in a tone that really meant, *what do you think you're doing in here?*

I explained that I was looking for a job. "The owner's not here, but there are no job openings." She shrugged.

"But won't you need more help during the summer season?"

She busied herself with arranging the clothing on the racks, then nudged me toward the exit.

My next stop was the Sidewalk Café, a small place with just two tables on the sidewalk and maybe a dozen more inside. The cafe mostly catered to takeout customers. I was told that there were no counter or server positions available but they needed someone to sweep up after closing. *No thanks!* I hoped I could do better.

I moved on to the A&P grocery store, where I knew they were in the midst of a summer hiring push for cashiers, counter help, stockers, and baggers. The store manager was a friendly guy named Mr. McFee. He knew my family and was always polite to my mother whenever I'd go shopping with her. I thought I had a good chance of landing a job there.

"Looking for a summer job. Can you help me out?" I asked, thinking that our family's connection would help.

"I'm sorry, son, we don't have any openings at this time," he said with squinted eyes and a clenched jaw.

"The season is about to start. When will you be hiring?"

Shifting his weight from side to side and avoiding eye contact with me, he said quietly, "We have no positions for colored people. I'm sorry. I don't make the rules. Good luck to you." He immediately turned and walked away.

It was like a gut punch. Even though I knew in my heart that being Cape Verdean was a huge strike against me, I never wanted to acknowledge it, because what could I do about it? I couldn't change my ethnicity to become more employable, more welcomed, more sought-after. I was born this way and would be Cape Verdean until the day I died.

Mr. McFee was the first person to say out loud what others were thinking and dancing around, with responses like; we're full, no openings right now, try us another time, or we're staffed for this season, maybe next year.

I proceeded to cover the rest of Main Street, Centre Street, Federal Street, Broad Street and even South Beach Street. I tried the fish markets, bicycle shops, cafes, restaurants, hotels, inns, gift shops, drug stores and mysteriously, at the end of May, just before Memorial Day and the start of the summer season, no one was hiring. Or perhaps I should say no one was hiring people of color to work in any customer-facing positions as white college students from all over the country descended on the island and easily picked up summer jobs—the ones I was told didn't exist.

Discouraged and ready to surrender to a summer of piecing together odd jobs, I was about to head home when I came across a boarding house on Pleasant Street called the Pleasant Inn. These days, it would be called a bed and breakfast, but they also served dinner. The owner was an elderly white woman in her seventies or eighties. As a teenager, she looked ancient to me. I remember she had very kind eyes and when she spoke to me, I felt she was talking to me and not at me, or worse, through me like I was an invisible man.

To my surprise, she offered me a position as bellhop and busboy. It was not all that I had hoped for but it was certainly a step in the right direction. The hours turned out to be perfect for me. The inn served breakfast and dinner, no lunch. That meant I had most of the day off to go hang out at the beach and I was done with my shift by 9:00 pm, in time to party.

I had a spring in my step as I headed home. I had a feeling this summer would be different somehow.

THREE

....

WITH EACH MEETING DANIEL WAS FEELING MORE comfortable with Anna, as if she were an old friend, maybe even a relative, with whom he could share tragic and tender stories. In preparation for her arrival, he dug up a folder he had kept. He hadn't saved much from his past, but there were some things he couldn't part with, like poems, articles, obituaries, and a piece of prose he had written in a moment of inspiration. As he leafed through his folder, he found the yellowing piece of paper with his handwritten words. When Anna arrived that day, they talked about the nor'easter that had ravaged their area a few days earlier and had leveled trees and branches.

"I darned near thought this place was going to blow away!" Daniel said. "It was enough to make a sailor weep."

Anna laughed. "And not much makes them weep."

"Oh, you've known sailors?"

She looked as if she was going to reveal something, and, instead, she said, "I can only imagine. The sea is a formidable friend and foe!"

"That it is," he said. His hand trembled slightly as he held his prose from so long ago.

"Do you have something for me?" Anna asked.

He nodded and handed her the piece of paper.

"What is it?" she said, looking down but not making sense of it.

"Read it. Will you, please?"

"Aloud, you mean?"

"Yes, if you don't mind."

"Sure." And she began.

"It is dark, the kind of darkness that obscures all vision. That is how it is on Commercial Wharf when the sun goes down and the moon doesn't come up. The town clock has just announced the arrival of midnight.

"A set of headlights pierces the darkness, approaching the scallop shanties that line the north side of the wharf. The 1935 Plymouth Coupe is moving at a snail's pace, as if reluctant to reach its destination.

"The vehicle creeps silently up the roadway. The only sound heard is the crunching of the tires as they pass over the scallop shells left stranded on the roadway, in memory of last year's scallop season.

"From October to January, the wharf bustles with activity, fishermen arriving before dawn, ready to make for the scallop beds before first light. They dredge offshore for scallops in the cold wet winter weather. This was back-breaking work. Activity continues throughout the day as the boats drift in once they have caught their limit.

"The afternoon and early evening are spent in the shanties, opening the scallops, and preparing them for market. Finally, there's the cleanup, collecting the shells and washing scallop guts from the benches and the floor.

"After sixteen hours, the fishermen head for home to rest and prepare to repeat the process the next day, and every day, for the brief season.

"This was the life of the driver of the 1935 Plymouth Coupe now parked, lights on, staring into the darkness, the abyss—the region of hell seen as a bottomless pit."

Anna looked up from the paper. "It's gorgeously melancholy and so evocative. Did you write this?"

Daniel nodded.

"What happened to the driver?" Anna asked almost in a whisper, as if she knew it was sacred and that she should tread lightly.

Daniel cleared his throat of phlegm but also of the memory lodged in there, threatening to reveal a part of himself he hadn't seen in a long, long time. He wondered if it even existed anymore.

I woke up early, as usual. The light shone through the hand-sewn blue and white ruffled curtains and raked across the wall. I just wasn't a sleeper. No matter what time I went to bed, my eyes popped open around 6:00 am. It was as if I didn't want the day to start without me, as if I would miss out on the best happenings if I slept in. So, I was always up and out of the house by 7:00 am, after grabbing a quick breakfast of plain toast and marmalade.

This was my last day off before I started work at the Pleasant Inn, my last day to hang out at the wharfs in the morning. I thought I might as well make the most of it. I loved checking out the boats, the gulls, and the people. I sometimes jotted things down in my notebook—thoughts, poetry, even occasional dreams. I gazed at the yachts moored in the harbor and wondered about the life of those on board, fantasizing about being wealthy. What was it like to be at sea in a floating luxury home—one that was much nicer than our actual home? If I were a yacht owner, would I smoke cigars, drink martinis, and order people around? Would I dress in a dapper suit and hat to match? Would I play card games with high stakes? Would I look down on townies with their sad little fishing boats?

I passed Boneka's and Riley's homes, but no one was stirring that time of day, which suited me just fine. Instead of going up Main Street, I decided to take the back way to the docks. I turned and strolled past the power plant on the no-name street. If the street had a name, I'd never seen a street sign. I just called it Back Street, even though there was another Back Street on the island.

I turned at the gas station heading toward the ice plant, where ice was made and sold to people on the island. Most Cape Verdean families had iceboxes. The ice was stored at the top and there was a pan on the bottom to catch the melting water. Back then, ice was a thriving residential and commercial business.

Whenever I passed the ice plant, I remembered crazy Ernie, the ice-plant man. When we were younger, my friends and I would swing by on muggy summer days to get shavings from large blocks of ice to melt in our mouths. Those ice shavings were pure heaven. Ernie would entice us to come inside and then lock the door on us! The first time it happened, we seriously panicked and thought we would freeze to death. But we soon learned he wouldn't keep us locked in for long. When he freed us, he would guffaw and slap his knee and carry on, thinking it was great fun. For us kids, not so much, but we tolerated his hijinks because that's how badly we wanted the ice shavings. It was the closest thing to ice cream we were ever going to get. Money was tight and not spent on extravagances like ice cream. It was reserved for essentials and sometimes there wasn't enough for that.

From the ice plant there was a clear view of the scallop shanties. As I peered down the road, I spotted Michael's Plymouth parked out front. *What is Michael doing down here so early in the morning?* I sped up, curious to see what Michael was up to. As I approached the car, I could see him in the driver's seat, his head tilted, awkwardly, back against the seat, asleep, but with the engine running. *Strange!* I tapped on the window several times to awaken him. After several failed attempts, I peered into the window to take a closer look and noticed white foam around Michael's mouth.

"Oh, God!" I cried, covering my mouth. I backed away from the car, my heart pounding in my head.

I knew that foam around the mouth was a sign of death from a book I had read. But I had never actually seen a dead person before. I hadn't envisioned death being so much like sleep. I froze, not knowing what to do, which way to go, whom to tell, or how to get help. Mostly I wanted to yell, *Help! My brother-in-law is dead! My sister Marie's husband is dead!* I quickly glanced around, but there was no one in sight. I had no idea what to do, whom to call. I just started running as fast as I could. I didn't know where I was going—home to tell my parents, to the police station, or to the fire station. I was just running to put distance between myself and that awful vision.

But then I questioned what I had seen. *Was my mind playing tricks on me? Had I actually seen Michael dead or was I imagining things? If he were dead, why, how? Did he have a heart attack? Had someone killed him?*

As I approached the gas station, I had to make a quick decision. *Should I turn left and run for home or turn right and go to the police station for help?*

I turned left. Kriolus didn't usually go to the authorities for any reason. Where Cape Verdeans were concerned, the authorities did more harm than good. We all knew they were just serving and protecting white folks.

My family gathered in our living room as two policemen with their rigid posture and stiff blue uniforms looked down at Marie. The tall, lanky one said, "Ma'am, I'm sorry to inform you that it appears your husband took his own life."

As if we didn't understand the meaning of 'took his own life,' the short, stocky one said, "Committed suicide."

I watched as her face froze in horror, the color draining from her cheeks. But I knew she wasn't going to let the police have the pleasure of seeing her fall apart. We were proud people and could be stoic when we needed to be.

The police couldn't leave quickly enough, and the minute they closed the door, Marie broke down. Mai attempted to comfort her with whispers, coos, and tender touch.

Everyone else sat quietly in total shock at the news. What do you say when someone you love chooses to go before their time?

"Mai, why would he do that?" Marie asked, wringing her hands.

"Se so Dios ki sabe," Mai said in Kriolu, looking skyward but not seeing God.

The old folks always reverted to speaking Kriolu when things were difficult to express in English. Even though I knew Kriolu, I couldn't always follow the entire conversation but I could get the gist. In this case, I knew, "God only knows," because old folks said it all the time. I guess they thought God was withholding all kinds of information.

"I knew he was upset that the town turned down his request for a license for his water taxi service, but I never thought it would come to this," said Pai.

Everyone knew that Michael and his father-in-law had worked hard refurbishing an old dilapidated party boat with plans to run an excursion service between Commercial Wharf and Coatue. Coatue was the strip of land that made up the outer perimeter of Nantucket Harbor. It was public land with a beach that no one used because it was inaccessible by land and far enough away by boat that few went there. Michael's idea was to set up a food stand on the peninsula, selling hot dogs and soft drinks and to shuttle people back and forth in his water taxi. It made for a perfect day-trip and a getaway from the crowded town beaches.

The town's fathers would have none of that. No colored was going to have such an exclusive and potentially lucrative business opportunity. Not on their watch.

Michael fought them as hard as he could, but they blocked him at every turn. They claimed his boat did not meet the safety criteria to carry that many people. They denied docking privileges due to the number of people projected to be on the docks. They said the use of Coatue for commercial purposes was against town ordinances. And the list went on. It wasn't the first time I had noticed that white folks had a way of making stuff up that sounded official to keep colored folks from having access to anything good.

Michael persevered, expecting that he would ultimately prevail. He poured his life savings into the project along with some of Pai's money.

When the final *no* was issued by the town council it was more than Michael could bear.

Daniel leaned forward in his wheelchair and gestured toward Anna. "You see, some people are better equipped to endure the slings and arrows of outrageous fortune. Michael had suffered from bouts of depression as a young adult, but in the 1940s little was known about this condition. A few decades before, people with depression were considered insane and locked away in sanatoriums—the insane asylums. Medical knowledge wasn't very advanced back then. It's not like now, where depression is viewed as a treatable illness, and there's less stigma."

Anna nodded. "Yes, we've come a long way since then. People suffered needlessly and were blamed for their conditions. Just think what antidepressants would've done for Michael."

Daniel glanced wistfully out the window. *If one weren't careful, one could drown in what could've been.*

I slumped on the couch and listened as the adults navigated the terrain of suicide. Death was bad enough without the added disgrace of suicide.

"What in heaven's name do I tell Michael junior?" Marie asked, mopping her bloodshot eyes.

"Tell him his father had a car accident and let it go at that," said Joseph, our older brother, who had just walked in after making funeral arrangements.

I wondered if the family could keep the news under wraps or if it would leak out. I certainly would do my part to keep the secret.

Joseph sighed and inhaled sharply as if preparing to deliver more bad news. "So, uh, Father John said we can't have a service in the church and that Michael can't be buried in the Catholic cemetery because, well because, he…committed suicide." He spoke the last two words quickly, like if he sped through that part it would make it less true.

Marie released a soul-searing scream, a depthless wailing that consumed her entire being. "Mother of God, what is happening? Why am I being punished? What have I done to deserve this? What did Michael do to deserve this? When will this persecution end?"

Her lamentation went on for a long time. Mai sat quietly beside her as there were no words in English or Kriolu that would soothe her pain.

In those moments, the world of adults seemed dreadful—like a dead end, a place where dreams died, an endless grind until death. No wonder some people chose not to wait for God. I hoped I would never enter that world and would instead remain forever young.

The wake, like all Cape Verdean wakes on the island, was held at the American Legion hall. As was customary, there was enough food to feed an army: chicken soup (canja), corn and bean stew (cachupa), a Portuguese pork stew (manchupa), beans and rice (jagacida), smoke-cured pork sausage (linguisa), flan (pudim de leite) and plenty of alcohol (grogue).

All the Cape Verdean families on the island came to pay their respects to Michael, who was well-known and loved. People whispered of his death and what they believed to be the reasons for it, the hushed talk of suicide. They mostly conversed in Kriolu so they could speak freely without worrying about being overheard by the children. It was somehow more comforting.

When Ava Pierce strolled into Legion Hall, I wasn't the only one who noticed her. Aunt Mabel and a group of ladies near me hushed and pretended not to stare. All attendees, including Ray Pereira himself, stopped talking, their eyes following Ava's movements through the hall. I glanced at Veronica, seated across the room with her parents and children, whose squinted eyes were fixed on Ava.

Cape Verdeans tended toward civility during community events. Feuds were set aside to bury the dead, celebrate a wedding, or the birth of a child. Today, at Michael's wake, I suspected no one would exchange harsh words, but that didn't stop Veronica from giving her husband, Ray, and Ava looks that could kill.

Ava was with her friend Angie Silva. Her head slightly bowed out of respect, Ava walked the gauntlet, politely acknowledging friends and acquaintances as she passed until she arrived at the Monteiros' table.

She reached out and took Marie's hand. They knew each other because Ava was Michael junior's teacher. Then, Ava stepped aside, giving Angie a chance to offer her condolences. After paying their respects, the two ladies headed for the exit, not stopping to partake in food or drink. Ava's head was bowed, but this time, she avoided eye contact as she clearly sensed that the room had eyes.

The minute the two ladies slipped out the door, the gossiping began.

I thought to myself, *this should be good,* and eavesdropped without being noticed—one of my well-honed talents.

"She has a lot of nerve coming here!" said a striking woman in a plain black hat with a veil. "Some people have no shame," said a petite lady in a bowler-style hat. Another who couldn't stop shaking her head said, "To think that Veronica…"

"Ladies, enough!" Aunt Mabel, the queen of the gossip, was quick to admonish them. "E ka ninhun dia nem tenpu," this is neither the time nor the place. There was no equivocation in her words or tone.

The women's eyes widened beneath their funeral hats, but they all clearly took my aunt's rebuke to heart. They resumed talking about poor Maria and Michael junior, left husbandless and fatherless.

When no one was looking, I snuck a little grogue. It wasn't the real, old country, stuff, just some cheap rum. It washed over me and made me feel lighter, freer, and almost forget. But the image of Michael in his car, his face contorted by death with foam around his mouth, was etched in my memory. Michael—a man with big dreams that crashed and shattered on the jagged rocks of Nantucket's shoreline, where so many of our peoples' dreams died.

FOUR

....

Daniel had been feeling blue. The only thing he had to look forward to these days were his visits from Anna. But for some unknown reason, he hadn't heard from her in a few weeks.

Are my stories uninteresting? Is she feeling like our sessions are a waste of time? I had warned her there wasn't much to tell at our first meeting. Perhaps she now agrees with me.

On this particular day Daniel had fallen asleep over a crossword puzzle that he had solved many times before, he was awakened by a knock-knock-knock. And a soft-spoken, "Daniel?"

He had been dreaming about eating a homemade rhubarb pie with Mai and Aunt Mabel, of all people, watching him. The rhubarb grew wild in Aunt Mabel's yard and she had caught him picking them without permission so they were making him eat the whole pie to teach him a lesson. The sweet sourness overwhelmed his taste buds. When Daniel was aroused, realizing he was still in his room at The Island Home and not under Aunt Mabel's dominion, he sighed.

"Daniel?" Anna said. "Is now a bad time? Should I come back later?"

"Oh, Anna. No, please, please come in. Pull up a chair!"

Anna told Daniel that she had to go off-island on short notice and had been unable to get a message to him before she left.

"Did you miss me?" she asked.

He started to respond when he saw she came bearing gifts, so he pretended he had not noticed her absence. "What have you got there?" Daniel could see Anna had something wrapped in tinfoil.

"I brought you something I know you're going to like," she said, beaming.

Daniel's eyes widened with anticipation. "Is that what I think it is?"

"If you think it's cuscus, you'd be right," Anna said, pleased with herself. "My aunt made it this morning."

Cape Verdean cuscus was like corn bread, made by steaming corn meal in a clay flour pot with cinnamon and sugar. It was eaten with butter or jelly or mixed with milk to make a cereal. Although it sounded simple, making it taste delicious was a lost art.

"I haven't had cuscus in ages! I won't tell you how long because you'll think N sta un bedjisa!" The occasion was worthy of a lapse into Kriolu, meaning *I'm an old fogie.*

Anna giggled like a schoolgirl.

He loved it when he tickled her funny bone. It made his week to see that he could brighten someone's day, especially a young lady as charming as Anna.

"Well, now that you're laughing, I know for a fact you think I'm an old fogie."

She touched his arm. "No, not at all. Old fogies are people who've run out of life. You're nowhere close to that, Daniel. Nowhere close."

Have I run out of life? Sometimes he felt like he had, but her visits made him feel alive again, like he had more life left in him, but he couldn't imagine what that meant.

He had been thinking of a tale he wanted to tell her about Roy Pina that happened following Michael's funeral, but it could wait just a little longer. Cuscus was a dish best eaten warm.

"I got some raspberry jelly from your favorite nurse." She reached into her purse and offered it to him.

After Daniel had thoroughly enjoyed his cuscus with a cup of herbal tea, he was ready to talk.

"I was going to tell you this when you first arrived but the cuscus was a wonderful distraction…" He paused to make sure he had her full attention. "We had some real excitement here last night. Norman Pratt, across the hall had a fire in his room." He pointed an arthritic finger towards the open doorway. "The fool left his hot plate on and went to sleep. It overheated and caught his room on fire."

"Those aren't allowed in here. Are they?" Anna asked.

"No, of course not. The man's a fool. I told you," Daniel said. "He almost burned this old place down. The original Island Home burned down in 1844. The whole joint's nothing but a tinderbox just waiting to go up in flames."

The vision of the place burning down made him chuckle to himself. *I can only hope. Set me free!*

He continued. "The fire alarm went off in the middle of the night and scared the bejesus out of me. I could'a had a heart attack." Seeing the stunned look on Anna's face, he smirked, "But I didn't."

"Anyway, I didn't finish telling you the story about what happened at Michael's wake." He bit his lip, not sure how to tell it, exactly.

"I don't know how much of this is true 'cause I heard it second-hand, but I'll let you be the judge." He paused and then corrected himself. "Well, I was actually there for part of it. I heard the men talking at the wake and Pai told me about the meeting they had at Roy Pina's. A bunch of us posted signs and marched up Main Street. The rest is hearsay from Pudgy Pina, but from what I know, it has the ring of truth."

ROY PINA

IT ALL BEGAN AT THE FUNERAL FOR MICHAEL MENDES.
A group of Michael's friends were grumbling about the town-fathers' treatment of Michael—the Selectman who had blocked Michael at every turn so that all his effort and investment were for naught, and he could see no way out.

"He did everything they asked to get his licenses and their approvals. But every time he did what they requested, the rules changed," said a man with a mustache and beard. "In other words, it was a moving target."

"He should have known they weren't going to give him the permits," said a tall, slender man with slicked-back hair.

"We need to do something about this, or it's never going to change," said a chubby man with hands on his hips, shaking his head.

"What can we do?" asked Joseph, Danny's older brother, looking defeated.

Roy Pina overheard them and interrupted. "This is not the time for this conversation. This is a wake. We're here to pay our respects to Marie and her family. Let's leave this conversation for another time."

They listened because Roy Pina was somebody, at least in their eyes.

Roy was 63 years old, his face deeply weathered as though he had earned every crease, every line, every furrow. The years of toil and trouble had taken their toll on Roy but had not dampened his spirit. The patriarch of the Pina family had 13 children and 27 grandchildren. He had a captive workforce and he managed his revenues carefully to ensure that his extended family prospered.

Roy Pina had the corner on the beauty market, setting up operations in the kitchen and parlor of various homes. Barbershops and beauty parlors didn't accept colored patrons. And coloreds were not allowed to open shops so Cape Verdeans used their homes to cut and style hair.

Roy also ran a night club out of a barn way out on Polpis Road. Everyone referred to it as 'the Barn.'" Along with the Barn there were a few shacks he rented out to Merkanus di kor in need of summer lodging. His son Pudgy ran his bookmaking operation.

The town police were aware of the unlicensed businesses and illegal night spot, but either they were on the take, or they decided to leave the natives be, as long as they were doing things out of sight of the God-fearing white folks. The Kriolus didn't know which and didn't care to ask.

Like so many others, Roy came to Nantucket with just the shirt on his back and toiled in the cranberry bogs. But, unlike others, Roy had two things working in his favor—he had an irrepressible entrepreneurial spirit and the strength of numbers. His pool of family resources included husbands, wives, and children, totaling 30. His oldest was 44, born when Roy and his wife Josephine were teens. Roy ran his family like a business and very successfully. In the Cape Verdean community, Roy was the elder statesman—the go-to person, the banker of last resort.

"Let's meet at my house at 6:00 pm Friday, and we can resume this conversation." Not waiting to be acknowledged, Roy crossed the room to rejoin his family.

Roy owned a large house on the corner of Primrose and Pine streets. In fact, his family owned several adjoining houses on that corner, where the in-home barber and beauty shops were also located.

That Friday, about a dozen men arrived at Roy's place and were invited into the parlor where some of the Pinas had already gathered. Josephine had laid out a pot of coffee and *pastel d'atum*, a delicious snack made of fried dough, tuna, onion, and spices. Roy served *grogue*, which meant alcohol in Kriolu. Grogue was also the name given to the national drink of Cape Verde—rum distilled from sugar cane with an alcohol content of 40 percent, a drink with the aroma of warm bananas. Of course, Roy had the best grogue, even though he didn't drink like Pai and many of the older generation.

As Roy made eye contact with the men in the room like a skilled public speaker, he wasted no time getting to the point. "You know why you came here tonight, but the question is what can we do to overcome this discrimination visited upon us by the white folks of Nantucket? Unless we have a voice on the Board of Selectman, nothing is going to change," he said, emphatically.

No one in their wildest dreams would have considered that a Cape Verdean could serve on the Board of Selectman. There were many town jobs at much lower levels that were out of reach for people of color: harbormaster, public works employee, town clerk, firefighter, and police officer.

"If we don't have someone in a decision-making position, decisions will be made for us and rarely to our benefit."

The men helplessly glanced at each other. They couldn't argue with this assertion nor could they do anything about it. They just waited for decisions to be handed down, ones that often had a negative impact on their community.

Roy stood up a little straighter with his head held high and said, "I'm going to run for the Board in the upcoming election."

Some men looked truly worried for Roy, others were inspired and in awe, still others shook their heads, believing that Roy would lose and nothing would change. But all were amazed by his audacity.

Elections for new board members occurred every June. Typically, it was a non-event for Cape Verdeans, but this year could be different.

After the shock of Roy's announcement dissipated, the men begin to talk excitedly, more openly, firing questions at Roy. "What can we do to help?" "What do you think your chances are?" "How's the town going to react to this?"

Roy told the group that he would need their support in posting flyers and organizing marches up Main Street and in front of Town Hall at 16 Broad Street.

The group came to life imagining the possibilities of what was unthinkable only moments ago. They became animated with the prospect of better jobs, better pay, and an easier life.

Roy noticed the excitement and enthusiasm in the voices of the younger men, while the older men in the group seemed less inclined to believe that anything would come of this. They had clearly depleted their supply of hope.

Before the meeting ended, Roy announced that his eldest son, Martim, would lead the effort and be in touch.

Within days, Roy had filed the necessary paperwork and Martim had people hang flyers around town.

As business manager of a sprawling number of enterprises, Roy had a regular daily routine, which included a nightly trip to the Barn to check inventory and collect receipts. As he turned off the dirt road that led to the Barn onto Polpis Road, headed for home, Roy reflected on the possibility of being elected to the Board. He knew it wasn't going to happen. He realized that this was a grand gesture, a warning shot, a notice to the town, that Cape Verdeans were not to be discounted. As he rounded a curve in the road, he noticed a vehicle oddly parked in the bushes in a slight turnout area. As he passed, he saw it was a town police car. They parked on this road periodically attempting to get speeders or drunk drivers returning home from the Barn. He paid it no mind until suddenly, a blue light flashed in his rearview mirror.

What is this about? I'm not speeding, swerving, or doing anything illegal, and more importantly, they all know my car.

Roy slowed his car, pulled over to the side of the road, slowed to a stop, and rolled down his window in anticipation.

"Get out of the car," the officer commanded.

Roy recognized the officer, Paul Schmitt, a diminutive man with a big presence and holster full of weapons.

"What's goin' on, Paul?" Roy asked, trying to appear calm.

"Just get out of the car," the officer said gruffly.

"What the hell's goin' on?" Roy asked again.

"Get out. Don't make me say it again," Paul yanked the door open and reached for Roy's arm.

"Back off. I'm getting out." Roy knew enough not to resist or to become confrontational. He was done talking with Paul, though. He'd wait until he arrived at the station and call his son, Martim.

"You're under arrest for a DWI. Just come along quietly."

Not only have I not been drinking. I never drink. The police know that.

Roy was handcuffed and shoved into the back of the police cruiser. He rode in silence to the police station with his head hanging low and with anger roiling in his gut. They arrived at the station around 11:00 pm. To his surprise, police Chief Wendell Woods was waiting for him. Police Chief Woods had red hair, a perpetual sunburn, and squinty eyes, like he was always being blinded by the sun.

"Take those cuffs off," the Chief directed.

Roy wasn't going to ask what this was about. He already knew. It had nothing to do with a DWI. He decided to remain silent and let it play out. He knew the Chief personally. They had an arrangement. He paid the Chief to look the other way regarding his various businesses that lacked the required licenses or permits.

"Look, Roy, this can go easy or it can go otherwise. It's up to you."

Still Roy said nothing. He didn't have much power in this situation, but he was going to make Chief Woods say it out loud.

"You know you can't win a seat on the Board of Selectman, so why are you running?" said the Chief, his arms crossed tightly over his chest.

Roy couldn't hold it in any longer. "If I can't win, what are you concerned about?"

"Your people look up to you. You're sending the wrong message. Uppity marches down Main Street and in front of Town Hall make folks uncomfortable. It's not good for the tourist trade. It just looks bad."

"Why is that, Chief?"

"Don't play games with me, boy..."

"It's Roy. Call me Roy. We've been doing this dance for a long time. You don't like what I'm doin', you tell me, but you call me by my name. I expected you folks would do something to wave me off, but I didn't think you'd stoop as low as arresting me on false charges." Roy inhaled sharply and shook his head.

"Let me make it perfectly clear. The town doesn't want you people interfering in town business. As long as you keep to yourselves, things will be fine. Have your little nightclub and other side businesses, but don't try to take it any further."

"Or else?" Roy knew he was treading on thin ice but he didn't care.

"Or else you'll be arrested for DWIs, your businesses will be shut down, and you'll end up like the rest of your kind—doing manual labor."

Roy sighed, paused briefly, and glared at Chief Woods. "Message received, Chief. I won't be running for the Board. I'm not a martyr. But fair warning, if you think I'm a pushover, think again. Our business arrangement is well-documented, so if I go down, you go with me and you have much further to fall." Unrestrained, Roy stood and strolled out of the police station, leaving the Chief to ponder Roy's remarks.

Word spread quickly about Roy's false arrest and the associated warning. This served its purpose to intimidate the Cape Verdean community. No one dared be so bold as to even consider running for the Board that year or any other year for a long, long time.

Roy wouldn't live to see the changes he pushed for. It would take nearly half a century before a person of color was elected to the Board of Selectman in Nantucket.

Roy had been 40 years too early. But at least he had tried.

FIVE

....

W HEN DANIEL'S FAVORITE NURSE, MONICA, CAME IN
one morning to administer his a.m. pills, he threw them down the
hatch and started clutching his throat, choking.

She shifted into gear, and in seconds positioned herself to administer the Heimlich maneuver.

Daniel said, "Gotcha!" and laughed heartily, slapping his knee.

"Oh, Mr. M, don't scare me like that!" Monica said, shaking her
head.

"Just thought I'd offer a little excitement around here. It gets
awfully dull. Don't you think?" Before Monica could answer, because he was afraid of what she might say, he asked, "Would you be
so kind as to provide me with a lap desk?"

"I thought you were going to say, 'lap dance,' and I was going to
report you for your dirty old man antics."

Daniel howled and Monica joined him in laughter.

"Seriously, whatcha need a lap desk for? Writing the great
American novel, Mr. M?" And Monica playfully poked his arm.

"Maybe. What's it to you?"

"Ah-ha! Now that you're being so cagey, I'm going to change
my theory. I think it's a love letter. Who's the lucky lady?" And she
tapped his arm again. "Do I know her?"

Daniel threw his head back in laughter. "Oh, Monica, the last time I was in love was… hold on a second. I have to do the math… was 67 years ago."

Monica's eyes widened. "A man as handsome and clever as you, staying single that long. I don't believe you. Let me guess. You were *that* picky. I know your type." Monica became quiet and serious. "That was the summer of '42. I'll bet there's a story in there." She gazed downward, clearly searching for the perfect words. "Did she break your heart?" she asked, tenderly.

Daniel averted his eyes. "Something like that."

She bent her knees to meet him eye to eye and placed her hand on his bony shoulder. "Oh, Mr. M, I'm sorry. I can tell you it was her loss. She walked away from a true gem."

He waved it away. "Oh, it was so long ago, I hardly remember."

"But sometimes those things can seem like yesterday. You know?"

How does she know that? She's far too young to know wistful heartbreak, Daniel thought.

Daniel knew that, unlike many of the nurses, Monica cared about her charges, especially him. Sometimes he wanted to tell her more, but she was so young, he didn't want to burden her with his past. One person burdened with his past was enough.

He patted her hand to let her know all was right with the world and she need not worry. "Now, about that lap desk."

"Yes, of course. Do you need a notebook and a fancy pen, too?" she asked.

"Yes, please. If you don't mind."

"Of course not. One lap desk, a notebook, and a pen coming right up!" she said as she held her index finger aloft and followed it out the door. She quickly did an about-face. "Every great writer needs a good cup of coffee. Would you like to pair your desk and writing materials with a nice cup of java?"

"I would love that!" said Daniel wondering how he had been so lucky to find Monica. He had heard horror stories about nurses in senior living facilities, but Monica was a dream come true. She was like the granddaughter he never had.

Daniel had been thinking about a story he wanted to share with Anna, one that had taken on a legendary quality on the island, one that had been told over and over again by Cape Verdeans for the heroism. He was sure in the telling and retelling, details had been added, embellishments, too, but the soul of the story was intact. Because his mind was sometimes foggy, he wanted to jot down the important details so he wouldn't leave anything out in the retelling. He wanted Anna to know that sometimes things can be turned upside-down in unexpected ways by people who have not forgotten what they have a right to, who've not forgotten their dignity. That sometimes people can't allow others to define their place in the world.

MADAME D'BOURVOIRE

SUMMER WAS IN FULL SWING. STEAMBOAT WHARF WAS
the disembarking point for summer visitors who planned to stay
longer than one day. The day-trippers arrived at Straight Wharf
coming from Hyannis, Massachusetts instead of New Bedford.

The Steamship Authority carried passengers and vehicles of
all kinds and was the lifeline between the island and the mainland. There to greet the high-end travelers were the drivers from
the various luxury hotels, men of color, dressed in uniforms that
resembled those of a doorman of an upscale Manhattan hotel.
Their appearance was quite out of place, inconsistent with the casual dress of visitors and locals alike, but it was the lawn jockey
blackface look that the hoteliers thought their patrons wanted to
see. The men were lined up at the end of the gangplank shouting
out the name of their lodging in a sing-song fashion, one after the
other.

"Hotel Breakers," "Harbor House," "Wauwinet House," "Seaside
Inn," "Palmer House." This chant was repeated until the last passenger had disembarked.

Madame D'Bouvoire and her family were one of the last groups
down the gangplank. She was traveling with her husband and her
two young daughters.

51

"Palmer House, that's us," she said to the driver, at the end of the line.

"Yes ma'am, right this way. Do you have any luggage?"

"Yes, there should be a luggage cart full of our bags."

When she said *our bags*, the driver looked up to see the three people behind her. It was obvious he didn't quite know what to make of the group.

Madame D'Bouvoire was French creole, another distinctive colored group. Her family was originally from New Orleans but her father moved them to Philadelphia to get away from the racist South.

Her Father, Percy D'Bouvoire was a chemist. He had developed a headache powder called Percy's Powder. Its effectiveness had made it a household name and was sold in every drugstore and pharmacy across the country. Most families had a bottle of Percy's Powder in their medicine cabinet. As a result, the family had become extremely wealthy.

His success was largely due to the fact that Percy appeared to be white with straight black hair, an extremely light complexion, and blue eyes. His daughter had inherited his traits, but her husband was darker and her daughters were in between. When Percy died, she took over the business and became one of the first colored female multi-millionaires in the country. When she married, she retained her maiden name, something not done in those days.

The driver hesitated for a moment, clearly not sure how to react to the situation: a white woman traveling with a group of coloreds. So, he collected their luggage and piled it into the back of the mini-bus. There were several white passengers already onboard as they entered the bus.

It was about an eight-mile drive from Steamboat Wharf to the Palmer House in Siasconset. There wasn't much to see on the ride once you left the town itself. There were stone mile-marks to delineate the distance and scruffy pine trees lining the roadway.

As the minibus crested the last hill before entering the village, structures dotted the roadside, many of them rundown, uninhabited rough-hewn shanties dating back to the 17th and 18th centuries when the village was first settled as a whaling outpost.

Siasconset was situated on a bluff with a clear view of the Atlantic Ocean. An 18th century visitor wrote, "Perfectly unconnected with the great world, and far removed from its perturbations." This was a perfect description of the village and the Palmer House, poised at the tip of the bluff with endless views of the sea.

The driver brought the vehicle to a stop in front of the covered entrance to the hotel and immediately began to unload the luggage.

The D'Bouvoires were the last on and first off, making their way to the entrance.

The driver watched as they entered, the look on his face a precursor of what was to come.

"D'Bouvoire party of four," she said cheerfully to the desk clerk.

The clerk looked at her, checked his reservation book, then looked at her again. "Ma'am, uh, you're welcome to stay here but your help are…"

"This is my husband and my daughters," she interrupted.

"I'm afraid this establishment does not cater to Negroes," he said timidly.

"I'd like to speak with the manager," she demanded.

"If you will please step aside so that I can help the others in line?"

"I'll do nothing of the kind. Get me the manager and do it now," her anger boiled over.

The manager came to the desk, looked at Madame D'Bouvoire, who from all appearances was white.

"What seems to be the problem, madame?" he asked very politely.

The clerk turned to his boss, covered his mouth, and conveyed to the manager that these folks were colored.

Immediately, the manager's tone and demeanor changed. "I'm sorry, we are not going to be able to accommodate you here."

"I did not realize that the 30-mile voyage across the Nantucket Sound has transported me to the Deep South. I thought this was Massachusetts, the state where Crispus Attucks, the first American and person of color to die in the Revolutionary War, gave his life for our freedom." Madame D'Bouvoire lashed out.

Her eloquent speech was lost on the manager. "I've never heard of a Mr. Attacks but it's a darned good name for a guy fighting in a war. Don't you think?" he said to the clerk, chuckling.

The clerk nodded a little too enthusiastically.

The manager puffed up his chest and glared at Madame D'Bouvoire. "Listen, I'm going to need to ask you to leave the premises promptly," he said, pointing to the door, as if she couldn't have figured out where the exit was. "You're not welcome here," he said sharply.

They were standing outside the Palmer House when the colored minibus driver meekly approached Madame D'Bouvoire's husband.

"Sur, if you're lookin' for a place to stay, Natty Turner has a boarding house below the bank. Just when you enter town, instead of takin' a right, you take a left, down the hill."

"Below the bank" was how the colored part of town was described. It was the only place where colored people were allowed to live in Siasconset. It was below the bluff and not afforded the protection of the bluff against the surging tides of a Nor'easter. Whenever a storm came, the properties below the bank would flood causing its residents to flee for higher ground. This was not a preferred circumstance but Merkanus di kor had no other alternative.

At Natty Turner's, the D'Bouvoire's were treated with dignity and respect. The rooms were small but they were clean and well kept. The cuisine was outstanding; local seafood was her specialty, but her menu also contained a number of Cajun dishes. Natty Turner had come to Nantucket by way of New Orleans and had brought the recipes with her.

If not for the invasive tide, Natty Turner's was a splendid location. It did not have the elevated views of the bluffs but did have the American beach grass that covered large sections of the beach in front of the property and the endless white sand that characterized Siasconset.

Madame D'Bouvoire returned to Philadelphia on a mission. She was going to show those racist Nantucket folks what it meant to disrespect Madame D'Bouvoire.

It took her several years, several attorneys and several million dollars, but she was finally able to purchase the Palmer House and she hired Natty Turner to run the place for her.

SIX

··

A NNA ARRIVED TO FIND DANIEL WITH A LAP DESK, writing furiously with a fancy pen. The only picture he had on his bureau was now sitting on the lap desk. He kept glancing up and smiling at it, as if the woman in the picture were in the room with him, as if it were an ode to her. Then he would write more.

"Good morning, Daniel," Anna said.

"It's actually afternoon," corrected Daniel.

"Oh, is it? Silly me," said Anna.

"Don't worry. You have better things to do than watch the clock. When you're stuck in a place like this, watching the clock is a bona fide activity."

Anna laughed.

Daniel suddenly became serious and held Anna's gaze. "Will you promise me something?"

"Sure," said Anna, clearly not knowing the promise but trusting him enough to agree beforehand.

"Don't get stuck in a god-forsaken place like this."

"Oh," Anna glanced down at her feet and then back at Daniel. "It doesn't seem so bad. People look after you and you don't have to cook," she said, trying to be upbeat.

"Well, you know what the other big activity is besides clock-watching?"

Anna didn't even have a guess.

"Waiting to die. We're all sitting here waiting for our number to be called by the Big Fella up there," he said, looking skyward. "I keep wondering when He's going to take me back to her." He held up Lisa's photo. "If I'm lucky, I'll find her again."

"Daniel, trust me. You're lucky."

"How can you be so sure?"

Anna put her hand on his shoulder. "Two souls knitted together across time and space are never really apart."

Daniel did a double-take. "Did you just come up with that or is that a quote from somewhere?"

Anna smiled shyly. "I just came up with it."

"That's how I've always felt."

"Tell me more about her."

There was an unnamed public beach at the end of Washington Street. Or at least I never knew the name. It wasn't very big, crowded in by the private homes lining the beach on one side and book-ended by a wall that blocked off a boatyard property on the other.

I wasn't sure why only a few tourists came to this beach. Perhaps the location and size weren't ideal. And the sand wasn't as nice as the out of town beaches or the Beach Street town beach. But it was convenient. And the good news was the locals had this beach to themselves and those locals tended to be Cape Verdeans. Like the beach, the rocky shore was full of shells, seaweed, and horseshoe crabs.

As I turned from Washington Street onto the beach, I spotted my cousins and their friends clustered in a group by the picket fence which delineated the private properties.

When I ran across the sand to greet them, I noticed a girl I had never seen before next to my cousin Terry Tavares. I didn't want to stare, but she caught my eye in her white, one-piece bathing suit, looking quite attractive.

I slid off my pants and shirt that I had worn over my yellow square-legged bathing suit so I'd be beach-ready.

I was suddenly self-conscious about my physique. Although I was toned from manual labor, I wasn't particularly muscular but neither was I unathletic. I chose a spot on the sand between my cousin Terry and the new girl. I dared to make eye contact and when she flashed a grin, I smiled back. I didn't know what my next move should be. I was overcome by shyness and awkwardly sat on my hands. *Why can't I be cool, calm, and collected? Should I ask her where she's from? Should I ask her what's she's doing here?*

Terry and the new girl talked across me, like I was invisible, but that was okay by me while I gained my composure. Of course, they were talking about guys they knew or were involved with and gossiped about girls. When they ran out of gossip, the conversation shifted to their plans for later and the past winter in New York.

Terry was a 20-year-old Nantucket girl. She left the island after graduation for the big city. There were no jobs on the island, no interesting men her age, and she wanted to add some adventure to her life. She had returned for a two-week vacation and would go back to the city, which she said was just fine with her.

"This island is Hicksville," Terry said with disdain.

"Oh, I don't think so. I think it's beautiful," said Lisa, her eyes sparkling.

"Beautiful, maybe, but trust me, it's so provincial and everyone is in your business. It's impossible to have any privacy. That's why I love the city. It's anonymous. The other thing—never get involved with a Nantucket guy. Ever!"

"Why not?" her friend asked.

"Oh, they're going nowhere fast. Because there's nowhere to go!" Her attitude was shared by most, if not all, Cape Verdean girls her age.

"I don't know. This place seems incredible." Then she turned to me. "Terry talked about summers in Nantucket so much, I had to come see it for myself."

"Hey, wanna take a dip?" Terry said to Lisa.

"Sure!" Lisa glanced at me, like *are you coming, too*? But it was clear Terry's invitation didn't include me. I could never understand what Terry had against me, but there wasn't much I could do about it.

The water in the harbor was warmer than the deeper ocean water, but it was still chilly when you first got in, so typically people would either run and dive in to get it over with, or they would wade in inch by inch allowing their bodies to acclimate. As a rule, guys usually dove and girls usually eased their way in, perhaps because girls were more sensible.

Terry and her roommate followed the tradition by easing their way into the water. I noticed they glanced at me a few times, which probably meant Terry was badmouthing me to her friend. My heart sank thinking that I had no chance with the cute girl. I mean, I thought chances were slim to begin with, but Terry probably ruined it for me.

The girls didn't really swim. They went out until the water reached their necks. They floated around and then came back to shore, talking all the while.

As they approached, Terry said, "Lisa wants to meet you. She thinks you're cute."

Lisa shot Terry a dirty look.

"I don't know why, but anyway, this is Danny Monteiro."

As we made eye contact, my mouth felt dry and my tongue heavy. I had nothing clever or smart to say.

"Hi, I'm Lisa Rivera. It's nice to meet you." Her whole face lit up and her dimples emerged like parentheses setting off her smile, accentuating her happiness.

Daniel paused and emerged from his reverie. "Anna, I'm sorry. I'm being a terrible host. Would you like something to drink? Perhaps prune juice or Miralax?"

Anna chuckled and wrinkled her face in disgust.

"The coffee's no good here but it does the trick if you'd like that. Doctor it up and you won't know the difference."

Anna nodded. "That sounds nice, actually."

Daniel wheeled over to his bed and pressed the red emergency call button. He wheeled back to face Anna.

Within seconds Monica came running into his room, panting, and looking panicked. But when she saw Daniel and Anna calmly sitting together, she said skeptically, "What's your emergency, Mr. M?"

"Coffee. Cream and sugar, please."

"Coffee is your emergency?" Monica flashed him a dirty-rotten-scoundrel look and shook her head. She couldn't help but smile, though. "You're bad, Mr. M. If you cry wolf too many times, you know what happens?"

He nodded with a mischievous grin. "Sure do. I have a life-threatening emergency, no one shows up, and I croak."

Anna and Monica cracked up.

"Oh, where are my manners? Anna, this is Monica, the nurse I drive crazy," said Daniel.

"We've already met Mr. M. I brought her to meet you. Remember? She turned to Anna, "Now, you keep him in line. You hear?"

"That's a tall order, but I'll try."

"I don't do this for everybody and don't get used to it. Two fancy coffees or just one?"

"Two, please," said Daniel.

Monica whizzed out.

"Where were we?"

"You had just met Lisa."

"Oh, yes, yes." He focused intently on a far-off place. "Why Lisa wasn't turned off by me at our first meeting was a question Terry would repeatedly ask Lisa. By all quantitative measures, Lisa and I were from very different worlds, but there was something else at work—the magic of chemistry. Attraction defies explanation.

"Lisa was a nineteen-year-old Puerto Rican girl from East Harlem, also known as Spanish Harlem. She was having an affair with a thirty-five-year-old married man, who was coincidently married to another Nantucket girl who had left years earlier for New York. Lisa was experienced, worldly, and not Cape Verdean.

"On the other hand, I wasn't much more than a child. It was a week before my eighteenth birthday and I was inexperienced when it came to women. My world consisted of Nantucket and the many books I'd read. New York, East Harlem and even New Bedford were like foreign countries to me.

"Lisa was five feet six inches about 127 pounds with a beautiful figure. She had high cheek bones, green eyes, full lips, and a penetrating smile—at least to me it was.

"I was six feet tall and barely 160 pounds soaking wet. I wasn't particularly handsome but I wasn't ugly, either. I was clean cut and youthful with straight black hair. Back then! Now I look like an old bald buzzard."

"Yeah, that's about right—a bald buzzard." Monica laughed and plunked the two coffees down in front of Anna and Daniel. They were served in glass mugs with whipped cream. "Mr. M, I spiked yours!"

"Oh, you tease," said Daniel.

Monica with her hands on her hips said, "Try me."

Daniel took a sip, swished it around, and said, "Damn, you're good. Irish coffee, my favorite."

"Thank you for the coffee!" Anna said as Monica turned to go.

"Sorry yours isn't spiked. I figured someone in here needed to stay sober," said Monica. "Have fun, you two!" And she disappeared.

"So, let's see… I was about to tell you the one noticeable thing Lisa and I had in common was skin tone. We were equally fair skinned.

"After that awkward day, something clicked between us. We met each day at the beach after I finished the morning shift and then again at night after my evening shift. We were two kids on the beach, chasing each other into the water, racing out to sea, and then frolicking in the occasional waves—jumping over, under and through—and body surfing. We'd dry off under the beating sun, and all the while I sneaked peeks at her gorgeous body. I was in a constant state of disbelief that she liked me. Really liked me. I could hear it in her laughter, see it in her flirty smile, feel it when she would rest her leg against mine or touch my arm when she laughed.

"This continued in spite of Terry's best efforts to scuttle our budding romance. Apparently, she would ask Lisa what she saw in me. She even brought up concerns about Tony, the married guy Lisa was seeing in New York, as if he had any ground to stand on. Terry was hell-bent on breaking us up. I didn't understand her motives. Perhaps she was friends with Tony Fonseka or just harbored a strong dislike for me. Lisa asked, and Terry said that she thought Lisa could do better than to get involved with a boy from Nantucket who was going nowhere with his life. She told Lisa it was the reason she left this place because of guys like me.

"The admonitions just rolled off Lisa's back or perhaps made her even more determined to pursue me. Ha! Lucky for me that my cousin's strategy backfired. She pursued me, which was a very good thing because I wouldn't have known the first thing about chasing her. All I can say is that I was under her spell. I was along for the ride, outclassed and outgunned. Being involved with Lisa was beyond my wildest dreams. She was pretty—very pretty. She was witty and worldly and I didn't know I was about to have the experience of my life."

I borrowed my older brother's truck and took Lisa out to Dionis Beach some evenings, where we could be alone. We would talk for hours and fool around a little. I didn't know how to take it to the next level and Lisa didn't want to have sex in the cab of a truck. So, our physical intimacy stalled while our emotional intimacy grew. On the one hand, I could hardly keep my hands off of her, but on the other, I was relieved because I was such a sexual novice and felt clumsy and embarrassed. Little did we know that help would come from an unsuspected source.

The Pinas ran a night club of sorts out of a barn, way out on Polpis Road. Along with the Barn, they rented out a few shacks to Merkanus di kor in need of summer lodging.

The police were aware of the illegal night spot, but either they were on the take or they decided to leave the natives alone, as long as we were doing things out of sight of the God-fearing white folks. I didn't know which and didn't care to ask.

One night, just to do something different, I took Lisa out to the Barn. We had such a great time listening to live music. It didn't take long for people to notice us. Men of all ages stared at Lisa and then looked at me with disbelief that said, *what is this kid doing with such a good-looking woman?* And they were bold enough to confront me.

Charles, a Merkanu di kor married to one of Aunt Mabel's daughters, approached our table with a swagger, like he owned the place. "Isn't she a little old for you?" He was a serious player. Marriage didn't stop him from going after anything with a skirt. "Hey, sweetheart, when you're ready for a real man, I'll be right here," he said to Lisa.

"I could be your daughter, old man," Lisa said matter-of-factly.

"But you're not," was his comeback, which he served with a creepy smile.

"But you're still old," she smiled tersely and turned back to me with will-he-please-go-away-now eyes.

He slunk back to his cronies who were watching him make a fool of himself.

Minutes after Charles tried to work his magic on Lisa, Sonya, a prostitute from just outside of Philly, approached us. Sonya had seen Charles come over to our table and make a fool of himself.

"What an ass!" she said, smiling and shaking her head. Then she leaned forward and whispered, "You two lovebirds need to get a room." She slipped into the booth beside us.

Sonya was in Nantucket for the summer to ply her trade, just making a living as best she could. She was dark-skinned, extremely beautiful, and voluptuous, a Nubian goddess. I had heard lots of stories about Sonya, what she was willing to do for a trick, how much she charged, and the quality of her work. I had heard she could make a young man weep and a grown man cry, which she probably did nightly.

But I had never spoken to her until that night. I had no idea where the conversation was heading. Was she saying this was no place for people our age or was she trying to rent us a room in one of the shacks out back?

Sonya clearly noticed the confused look on my face. "Kids, look. I can see that the two of you are in love. You shouldn't be in a dump like this. I have a place out back. The key is under the mat." Sonya nodded her head in the direction of the door. "Now, go and have a good time."

Sonya left the booth as quickly as she came.

We glanced at each other, and without saying a word, we were out the door. I was such a bundle of nervous excitement I couldn't get the key in the keyhole. Lisa took it from me and unlocked Sonya's love shack. The place was a bit ram shackled with some faded posters of beach scenes on the wall, a small kitchen and seating area and a bedroom at either end. Without giving it a second thought we migrated to the closest bedroom.

I'd like to say it was pure magic from the moment we kissed, but once we started making love, I went quickly. To my dismay, I didn't last more than a minute, if I lasted that long. Afterwards, we cuddled and shared secrets. My lack of sexual prowess could have ended our romance, but Lisa was gentle and patient with me, her young inexperienced lover. She passed it off as no big deal, nothing concerning.

I still worried, though. I worried that it would be the end of us. In the days that followed, it became the elephant in the room for me. If it was an issue for Lisa, I never knew. With her subtle coaching and patience, I learned how to breathe and relax into our lovemaking when I thought I couldn't hold on any longer.

Lisa and I frequented Sonya's shack but never without her permission. She never asked for anything in return. Initially, she didn't even ask for our names. Sonya did this out of the kindness of her heart, perhaps remembering a time when she herself had been young, innocent, and in love.

SEVEN

"**D**O YOU HAVE TIME FOR ONE MORE?" ASKED DANIEL, who felt like he could almost feel his legs again—the ones that took him to the beach and into the water for a dip, the ones that sensed the soft sand beneath them, the ones that felt the cool rain when he got caught in a downpour, the ones that raced home when he was late for dinner, the ones that intertwined with Lisa's silky legs and never wanted to let go.

Anna checked her iPhone. "I sure do."

"Are you sure I'm not putting you to sleep?"

"Daniel, I love your stories. I love traveling back to a time that will never come again, to a time that lights up your face, to a time where I can see Danny in you."

Daniel blushed. He hadn't realized Anna felt anything for him. He thought she might just be politely enduring his tales for her research. He wanted to thank her for caring but he didn't want to draw attention to something that might be fleeting. He didn't want to scare it away.

"I've got one about my brother, Joseph. Let me see if I can describe him to give you a picture. He was my oldest brother and neither handsome nor ugly, more the character actor looking type. Joseph was five-nine with a medium build, and physically fit as a result of all his manual labor. He was a quintessential Cape Verdean. We always say we can tell a fellow Cape Verdean on sight, although we come in many shades, from white to black. There's a commonness to ours features, clearly discernable by those who know what to look for."

JOSEPH MONTEIRO

Sarah and Joseph were into it again.

She followed him around the house, screaming at his back. "You're a weak little man. The Forsyths treat you like a boy and you just take it," said Sarah.

"What do you want me to do?" asked Joseph.

"Be a man. Stand up for yourself, that's what."

"And lose my job and then what?"

"That's your problem. People just walk all over you. You have no backbone. What are you so afraid of?"

He stopped in the living room, twisted around, and yelled, "Shut up!"

"Make me! You weak little Cape Verdean excuse for a man," she said, each word dripping with venom.

Joseph attempted to deliver a quieting blow to Sarah's mouth. But Sarah was a big woman, six feet tall, hefty at 193 pounds and solid as a rock. She blocked Joseph's punch with her hand, snatching his fist out of the air and twisting his arm like a pretzel.

As he reeled back in pain, she returned his scuttled attack with a punch, but unlike Joseph, she made contact squarely with his face, knocking him to the floor.

She stood over him and said, "You best stay down there because if you get up, I'm going to beat you like I own you."

Subdued, Joseph remained where he fell. Sarah turned her back on him, picked up her unfinished drink off the coffee table and unceremoniously drained the glass.

This was not an isolated incident for Joseph and Sarah, they fought often and the fights were often loud and boisterous. But the escalation to physical violence was new and a harbinger of things to come.

Their lives had not always been like this. There had been happier times. Twelve years earlier, when they first met, Sarah was working for the Tobys. The family had a summer home in Surfside, on the south shore of the island.

The Tobys were in the garment business making pajamas. They had an apartment in The Dakota, one of the oldest and most luxurious buildings in Central Park West. Their upscale lifestyle was possible because everyone wore pajamas.

The Tobys were Jewish. They had changed their name from Tobias to Toby, as was the custom of many Jews during this period trying to disguise their heritage. Like everyone, they wanted to be absorbed into the melting pot of white Christian America, the criterion for being able to enjoy *white privilege*.

Sarah Turner was a live-in domestic and traveled with them summers when they came to Nantucket. Sarah had met Joseph her first summer on Main Street, without introduction.

Thursday was maids' day off, an unspoken custom. All the colored help had the same day off and they would flock to Main Street on Thursdays to occupy the public benches. There wasn't much else for them to do and nowhere to go. Their recreation on their only day off consisted of sitting, talking to one another, and watching the people go by.

Sarah had caught Joseph's eye as he plodded up Main Street to his job at the Five and Ten, the local general store. They made eye contact and exchanged smiles, but Joseph kept walking. While at work, the vision of Sarah stayed with him. But, by the time he left work that day, Sarah was nowhere to be found.

Joseph waited impatiently for Thursday to roll around. He was on a mission to meet this woman. He didn't know her name and it wasn't the custom for Cape Verdean men to socialize with Merkanas di kor, colored women who were not Cape Verdean, but he didn't care.

It took another week before he would encounter Sarah again, sitting on that same bench, alone. Joseph plopped down on the bench beside her and they exchanged glances. Joseph bent down pretending his shoe was untied and that he only stopped to remedy the situation. But he was not leaving without finding out who she was.

"Are you from the island?" Joseph asked, knowing full well that she wasn't. The population of people of color on the island was so small that every person of color knew every other, if only by sight.

"No," Sarah replied, "just here for the summer."

Perfect, Joseph thought, *this is my opening.*

"So, what brought you here?"

They talked for a while, Sarah sharing her situation with Joseph. He learned her name, who she worked for, where she was working, and then realized he had to get to work.

He clumsily asked if they could meet later. Sarah, who knew no one else on the island besides the Toby family, welcomed the offer.

They spent the remainder of the summer's Thursdays together. Joseph took her all over the island in his truck, much of that time spent at Dionis Beach, where locals went to party, make out, and have sex.

As Labor Day approached, the Tobys prepared to pack up and leave for New York. Joseph and Sarah said their tearful goodbyes. Summer romances were not uncommon for Nantucket Island; in fact, they were the norm. People were brought together by circumstance, enjoyed each other for a few months, and then went on with their lives.

But in early October, when the moors were laced with autumn colors, Sarah disembarked from the ferry at Steamboat Wharf into the welcoming arms of her summer lover.

"I never thought I would see you again," Joseph said, drinking in her beauty.

"Don't be so melodramatic. I was coming back next summer," she said, smiling. "But I couldn't wait."

Sarah found a job at the laundry and some part-time domestic work as well.

"You can't bring that Merkana di kor into this family," Marie said. Our father and mother were thinking the same but they were more passive-aggressive in dealing with the situation, giving Sarah the cold shoulder, not including her in conversations and speaking Kriolu to each other in her presence.

Within a year, Joseph and Sarah married over the protestations of our family.

It took time, but ultimately Sarah was accepted into our family. But as the years passed and their marital relationship deteriorated, old resentments resurfaced.

"I told him he shouldn't have married that Merkana di kor. See what happens?" said Marie.

When used in this fashion, Merkana di kor was a pejorative term used to denigrate people of color who were not Cape Verdean.

Joseph worked for David Forsyth who owned several business-es on the island including the Five and Ten. The Forsyths had a sprawling property off of Hummock Pond Road. In addition to working at the Five and Ten, Joseph was the Forsyths' handyman. Whenever Barbara Forsyth needed errands run, she would call on Joseph. He was literally at their beck and call, but it was steady work so he wasn't complaining.

The Forsyths had a young daughter, Jane, who took after her mother and enjoyed bossing people around and getting her way.

Barbara Forsyth wasn't a Nantucket native, quite the contrary. She came from a wealthy family from upstate New York and ini-tially came to the island reluctantly after marrying David, whose family had been here for generations. She quickly adapted to life as the wife of a country squire, thanks to their social status as mem-bers of the Sankaty Head Golf Club and the Nantucket Yacht and Tennis Club. This was a world beyond the reach of any person of color on Nantucket and as alien as life on the moon. Danny had seen the inside of the golf club only once as a caddy.

Barbara felt entitled and made those of lower social standing feel that distinction in unnecessary and petty ways. Joseph was her preferred target.

"Joseph, you did a terrible job painting that fence. Where are the potatoes I told you to pick up at the store? How many times do I have to tell you not to park your truck there?" *You people* was one of her constant phrases. "You people need to know your place. You people can't seem to do anything right. You people... You people."

David Forsyth was less confrontational but he catered to his wife's and daughter's wishes at Joseph's expense, making him do things just to please them.

"What happened to you?" said Marie, staring at Joseph's black eye. Joseph had stopped by our parent's house, as he did daily. It was a matter of respect, something that Cape Verdean children did no matter how old they were. They stopped by to say hello and check in.

He ignored Marie's remarks.

"Where are Mai and Pai?"

"Pai is down at the wharf working on that damn boat. Mai went with Aunt Mabel to see about some work at the Stetson's Inn."

"You want to talk about it?" she asked, staring at his swollen eye.

"Sarah and I got into it. That's all."

"Is she going to show up with some black-and-blues?"

Again, he ignored Marie. "Tell them I stopped by and I'll see them later."

"Good thing you guys didn't have any kids," she shouted after him as he slipped out the back door.

"What happened to Joseph's eye?" asked Jane, the Forsyths' seven-year-old daughter. Back then, children referred to adults by their surnames, but that deference was not afforded to people of color.

"It appears he got into a fight with someone. You know how those people are." Barbara rolled her eyes.

"Joseph, Jane tells me your nephew was bothering her in the school yard the other day. Speak to him and make sure that it stops."

The accused was Marie's son Michael Jr., who was just seven years old.

"What did he do?" asked Joseph.

"Never mind that. Just speak to him and make sure it doesn't happen again. Am I clear?"

"I'll speak to him."

The Forsyths' constant humiliation and challenges to Joseph's self-worth as well as the restrictive social norms imposed on people of color by Nantucket's white population was enough to drive any man to drink. Combine that with the isolation of winter, the shortage of off-season work, the lack of any social outlet and the loss of respect Joseph felt from Sarah, he desperately needed relief.

When winter set in with its short days and long nights, the bone-chilling cold, countless hours to kill, Joseph reached for alcohol, the lubricant that smoothed the abrasive edges of daily life. He wasn't alone. Alcoholism was pervasive in our community.

Although Joseph drank heavily, he never boozed during the day and never went to work reeking of alcohol. But his drinking was clearly taking a toll on his physical and mental health. He no longer had the endurance of his youth. He was quick to anger and to take his anger out on Sarah. He had become a shell of his former self.

Sarah was also a functioning alcoholic, carrying her nips in her purse and sipping from them at every opportunity.

It was all about coping the best they could.

Marie was in the living room with Mai when she heard her son Michael Jr. cry out.

"I'm telling my mother", and he came running into the room from the kitchen to his mother.

"Ma, Uncle Joe, hit me in my head," he said, holding the top of his head with both hands. Marie was up in a flash, making it for the kitchen doorway, as Joseph stepped into the living room.

"What are you doing, hitting my son? Don't you ever put your hands on him! What wrong with you? You been drinking or something?"

"The kid needs to learn to keep his hands to himself," Joseph said trying to justify his actions.

"What are you talking about?"

"Ask him what he did to Jane Forsyth. Go ahead, ask him."

"What's your uncle talking about?" She challenged Michael while keeping a disapproving eye on her brother Joseph.

"I didn't do anything to her. All I did was give her a picture that I drew."

"Why'd you do that?" Marie asked calmly.

"Because I like her."

Michael had no clue about the undercurrent of bigotry that exists on the island. He didn't know he wasn't supposed to like Jane Forsyth, let alone show it in any way. Cape Verdean's didn't give their kids "the talk." You grew up and figured it out for yourself by observing others.

"Did you hit or touch her in any way?" Marie pressed.

"No, Ma, I like her that's all." He began to cry, not at all sure what was happening.

Marie turned her attention to her brother Joseph.

"So you come in here and whack my son on the head based upon what some white girl said without finding out your nephew's side of the story? Is that what you're telling me?" Marie was all up in her brother's face.

"If you ever hit my son again, for any reason, so help me, I'll..."

That's as far as Marie got before Mai intervened.

"Stop it right now. What's wrong with you two?" She turned to Joseph.

"Pai and I taught you better than that. El e bo familha," he's your family, she said staring Joseph down and then glancing toward Michael Jr.

Feeling cornered, Joseph turned to Michael, "Sorry, for hitting you, but stay away from Jane, she doesn't like you back."

Hearing those words, Michael Jr. was crushed and went running out of the room.

Marie had had enough of her brother. She shooed him out of the room.

"Go home."

No more words were spoken as Joseph walked across the room. He kissed Mai on the cheek as a gesture of apology, glowered at Marie, and then he left.

"It's a sad world we are living in when kids can't even play together," said Mai.

"It's always been like that, Mai, brankus and Kiolus keep to themselves."

Mai said, "It's time for you to have a talk with Michael Jr."

Marie acknowledged with a knowing sigh.

EIGHT

....

DANIEL HAD BEEN TALKING FOR A WHILE. ANNA COULD see that he was misting up as the story became more personal.

"Would you like to take a break?" she asked.

"No, I'm fine," he said, but Anna looked skeptical.

"Would you like some water or something to drink?"

"Any chance you brought some whiskey for your favorite curmudgeon?"

"It's against the rules. Isn't it?"

"Well, at this age if you break the rules, what can they do? Throw you in the slammer? How's that different from this place?"

She laughed. "On the rocks or straight up?"

"Oh, on the rocks, of course. It's much better chilled."

"Be right back," she said. "Of course, I won't tell them what the rocks are for."

"Good call!"

Anna disappeared on her ice-seeking mission, leaving Daniel alone with his thoughts.

He peered at the framed photo of Lisa Rivera sitting on his dresser. It captured her in a moment of pure joy when she belonged to him. For 67 years, she had remained that way, young, carefree, and willing to take a chance on him. To think otherwise would have been a betrayal. But his mind drifted there without his consent. *Who did she become? Did she find love again? Did she marry and have a family? Was she truly happy? Was she still alive? Could he possibly find...?*

Daniel wouldn't let himself finish his last thought. Each question pricked his heart more than the previous. As a goodhearted man, he should've wished Lisa all the happiness in the world, but he held out hope that she, too, had never fully moved on. That she, too, was frozen in time, pining for her one true love.

A wave of sorrow crossed his face and weighed down his body. Tears pooled in his eyes, but he blinked them away. He had not thought about her this deeply for many, many years. He often looked at her picture but it was always just a fleeting glance. He never dared to stare at it fearing a flood of emotions, memories he thought were lost forever, now so vivid, and clear. It was like they happened yesterday.

Anna returned carrying a glass of ice. She noticed the crestfallen look on Daniel's face but she clearly knew not to acknowledge it.

She pulled the bottle of whisky from her purse and poured the gold liquid over the ice.

"Ahhh! I can smell the divine scent from here," Daniel said, closing his eyes.

"If I give you this, you're not going to let on that I brought in some bootleg. Are you? You could get me kicked out of this place."

"Oh, heck, no. I'm such a good undercover drunk." He chuckled. "Had lots of practice. You sober up real quick when the cops come. They cut Cape Verdeans no slack. Probably still don't. If I start slurring, you can pour a bucket of cold water over my head."

Anna giggled. "You may see yourself as a curmudgeon, but you're a comical curmudgeon."

"Hey, I'll take it! I think that's the nicest thing anyone has ever said about me."

"Oh, I doubt it. Your curmedgeonliness, if that's a word, is just bluster to throw people off your scent."

He peered at Anna skeptically. "And what scent is that?" he asked, taking a long sip of his whiskey on the rocks.

"Your tenderheartedness."

"Oh, damn! Is it that obvious?"

Anna nodded. "Sorry if I wasn't supposed to notice."

Daniel blushed and glanced down at his feet, his feet that had once chased after things, his feet that were useless now. The last time they could carry him, she was still his and he was hers.

He leaned forward and said, "You won't tell anyone. Will you?"

Anna shook her head. "Mum's the word. It's our secret." She pantomimed locking her mouth and throwing away the key.

"Now, where was I?"

"You were telling me about your brother, Alfred."

"Ah, yes."

My brother Alfred—or Freddie as everyone called him—and I were headed to the dump.

Freddie had the darkest complexion in the Monteiro family. It probably came from Mai's side. Though she was extremely light complexed, her mother was Azorean, her father Peter Vieira was from the island of Fogo and was dark as coal. Freddie wasn't quite that dark, he had straight black hair and smooth skin and could easily be mistaken for East Indian.

We planned to swing by Joseph's to see if he had any trash to add to the pile we had already loaded in the back of the truck.

The town had no sanitation department. There were private contractors that could be hired to pick up your trash but it was cheaper to make a periodic free trip to the town dump, which was a little way out of town off of Madaket Road.

"The Merkanus di kor are making it hard for us Cape Verdeans. You know, the way they act all subservient around white folks." Freddie's tone was disparaging.

"You know that Cape Verdeans are Merkanus di kor, too," I said. "When the Portuguese settlers discovered the Cape Verde Islands off the west coast of Africa, they mixed with the slaves who were brought over from Senegal."

We had just turned onto Francis Street from Washington Street, approaching the stop sign at the T in the road.

Without warning Freddie released the steering wheel and grabbed me by the throat with both hands, squeezing hard. "God damned know-it-all! Take that back," he yelled, while violently shaking me by the neck. "Take that back!"

I struggled to breathe and desperately tried to shake him off. "Let go, Freddie! Let go!" I said, my words a hoarse whisper.

Freddie snapped out of his fit of fury, let me go, and grabbed the wheel as the truck veered toward the curb.

I gasped for air. "Jesus, Freddie!" I was shocked that a casual remark would elicit such a violent response and that my brother would choke me because I implied we were Merkanus di kor. Although Cape Verdeans saw themselves as different from other colored people, it was in name only. Kriolus had a distinct language and a country of origin, Merkanus di kor, as a rule, had neither.

We traveled in silence for the remainder of the ride, neither looking at the other, and no apology offered. Forgiveness wasn't a consideration.

I thought about my brother's words. It wasn't the first time someone called me a know-it-all, which made it all the more confusing that my cousin Terry thought of me as a dolt. Saying I was well-read might have been a stretch but I had read more than a few books. Winters in Nantucket, especially for Cape Verdeans, offered few diversions. Alcohol was one, but I was too young for that. That left only the library as an escape from the dark, dreary days, where the ocean and the beach were useless and the island was dead. Only the people with no other choice remained.

I had read many of the classics: *Ivanhoe*, *Moby Dick*, *The Three Musketeers*, and the like. I read what little I could find about the Cape Verde Islands and its people, the rise of the indigenous slave trade and the diaspora that had brought my family to America.

Then I turned to reading about world religions, which eventually led me to parapsychology. My interest caused me to pay a visit to Margaret Santos, the gypsy, on Washington Street. It was like she could see the future in her cards. The last card she pulled was the Ten of Swords. She inhaled sharply and shook her head.

"What? What is it?" I asked. I peered down at the card to see a man lying face down with ten swords in his back. A chill rippled down my spine. It didn't look good at all.

85

She held my gaze and said, "Something unexpected will happen and your life will never be the same. A tragedy of sorts."

What kind of tragedy? My heart was racing. I made up an excuse that I was late for dinner and nearly sprinted out of her spooky supernatural house, praying all the while that her cards were nonsense. That was enough to make me return to reading fiction.

I had only a high school education, but because I loved learning about many different things, my knowledge base was wide, not deep. I was a Jack of all subjects and a master of none! This probably kept Lisa interested in me. She marveled when I talked about the history of Cape Verdeans, and in the same breath, institutional racism, and racist themes in literature, citing Langston Hughes. She would often remark that I seemed wiser than my years. Of course, because I was young and insecure, I often felt like an imposter, like I didn't know much about anything. Lisa made me feel clever and like an excellent communicator. When I was with her, I thought maybe I could be a professor, a lawyer, or even a novelist. I could imagine myself standing in front of a lecture hall, sharing my insights and knowledge, or pacing in front of a courtroom, making my compelling closing argument. I could see myself in a writer's studio peering up from my typewriter, gaining inspiration from the whitecaps in the steely-gray sea. The magic of her presence made me dream big!

This was perhaps the very quality that Terry disliked in me— that she saw me as a cocky know-it-all. It was easier for her to think of me as a dolt than attempt to compete intellectually.

Intellect wasn't a cherished commodity in the Cape Verdean community. The focus was more on survival. Manual labor skills were the measure of a man. Could you fix a motor, repair a lobster trap, restore an old boat, build a shed, or mend a fence? If you could, you were sought-after. I could do none of those things. Even worse, I had no interest in learning any of those skills. This was a growing concern, especially now that I was out of high school. *What would I do with the rest of my life?*

I liked to write, poetry mostly. But I didn't dare reveal my secret or show my work to anyone. And I had no idea how I could make a living writing. I kept my journals hidden under my mattress and was sure to move them on laundry day when Mai would change my sheets.

I first got the idea to become a writer when I found a reference to Langston Hughes buried inside an old Reader's Digest. I read about Langston Hughes and how he had gone from Joplin, Missouri, to New York to become a famous poet, playwright, and novelist. He had attended Columbia University. I had to send away for a copy of one of his books, because the Nantucket library did not acquire books written by coloreds.

The book, *The Ways of White Folks*, was a collection of 14 short stories about race relations. My favorite was "Cora Unashamed," a portrait of an isolated black woman in a small Midwestern town, who stoically survived her own sorrows, but in the end lashed out against the hypocrisy of the whites who employed her. I could identify with its theme, wishing I could lash out against the hypocrisy that surrounded me.

"Passing," hit even closer to home. It was the story of a colored man passing for white. On Nantucket, if you passed for white, doors opened for you magically, but if, in the case of the Limas, you passed for white, but people knew you were not, it was a different story.

I clearly remembered the day Cory Lima and his sister Genie came to see my mother. I sat in the living room quietly pretending to play while they talked. Cory and my brother, Junior, were close friends growing up. They did everything together, played together, got in trouble together, learned to swim together, but as they got into their teenage years, they grew apart.

Cory and his sister looked as white as any Caucasian with straight hair and blue eyes. If you saw them on the street by themselves, you would certainly take them for white, but their parents were Cape Verdean, their family and friends on the island were Cape Verdean, and they were known by the whites on the island as Cape Verdean. Therefore, they were afforded the same treatment as any other Cape Verdean despite their light skin tone.

"Da en benson," said Cory to my mother. It was a Cape Verdean custom to ask your elders for their blessing, as a greeting.

"Abensua nhos," bless you both, she replied.

Cory was asking for my mother's blessing because what he was about to tell her was breaking his heart and he knew it would break hers as well. The Limas, the Vieiras, and the Monteiros had been very close for three generations.

"Genie and I are leaving Nantucket and we won't be coming back. We can't make a life for ourselves here on this island. There are just no opportunities for us."

My mother's face drooped in sorrow. She knew exactly what they were talking about. She had endured the racism in silence. It was how her generation had survived.

She remembered the times when there was no work, little food, and even less hope. These young kids had a chance for a better life, away from this island, where they could be brankus, where no one knew they were Cape Verdean, where no one would keep them down because their blood was somehow *tainted*. She would not hold that against them.

Cory and Genie lingered, talking with my mother about happier times. They drew out the visit, because once the conversation ended, they would be out of our lives forever.

When they were all talked out and cried out, Mai said, "Dios ba ku nhos," God go with you both.

They each replied, "Dios fika ku bo," God stay with you.

I had heard this exchange of salutation many times but never had it resonated so profoundly.

Freddie pulled into Joseph's yard and parked with a jerk. I immediately stepped out of the truck and turned back toward the road. Freddie knew better than to say anything to me. I was sure he felt bad about choking me but could find no words of apology. There was no way he'd concede to being Merkanu di kor. No way.

My dinner shift was due to start in a few hours, and I so badly wanted to see Lisa. She was someone I could talk to about what happened with Freddie. She understood me. She had just one week of vacation remaining before she had to return to New York. I wanted to make every remaining moment count.

NINE

··

AVA PIERCE

No EVENT OR ACTIVITY EVER STANDS ALONE; EACH is linked in an unbroken chain of preceding and cascading events. So it was with Ava Pierce and Ray Pereira's decision to move in together. The news spread through the Kriolu community, stoked equally by gossiping women and whispering men faster than a wildfire during a thirsty summer.

It took little time for word of Ava Pierce's perceived indiscretions to reach the Nantucket schoolboard by way of the nosy white folks who maintained the town's social order. In a small town like Nantucket, three members made up the schoolboard— Superintendent Robert Mitchell, Principal David Morse, and William Gentry, a guidance counselor.

To address their concerns about her conduct and how it reflected on the school and the town, Ava was called before them. They were meeting at Cyrus Peirce Elementary School. Though not related, their names spelled differently, and they lived a century apart. Ava and Cyrus shared many of the same views on education and equality.

Cyrus Peirce was a renowned educator who managed private and public schools on Nantucket and the greater Boston areas. He was instrumental in creating the University of Massachusetts, fought for equal education for boys and girls of all races, and worked with the abolitionist movement. Ava knew his story, admired his courage, and was determined to be equally courageous in her own way.

Ava was neither attractive nor unattractive. She was petite and 5'5" with a pleasant appearance, light brown hair, brown eyes, and a pale complexion. At the beach, Ava had to cover up, or she would become a lobster in a matter of minutes. She loved children and her job teaching them.

From Main Street, Ava had walked up Academy Hill to the school to clear her mind and prepare her message. When she entered the room, the board members were already seated. The room was stuffy, and a stale odor permeated the air. She was invited to have a seat at the head of the table.

"Please, help yourself to a donut," said William Gentry, in a half-hearted attempt to be cordial.

Ava shook her head. "No, thank you."

Without introduction, Superintendent Mitchell began. "It has come to our attention that you…"

"Let me stop you right there." She made eye contact with each of the men as she spoke. "First of all, what I do in my personal life is none of your business as long as I am committing no crime or doing anything immoral."

"Do you consider it moral to be living with and consorting with colored people? It reflects poorly on you and your upbringing, to say nothing of the school and the town," said Superintendent Mitchell.

She let him finish his thought because she wanted to see how prejudiced people acted when they were among like-minded bigots. "You would be advised to leave my family out of this discussion..." Ava said defiantly. "What is wrong with you people? Where are your Christian values? Don't answer that. I know where they are. You—all of you." She looked around the room, glaring at each of the board members in turn. "Conditional, convenient Christians, all of you. You presume to tell me what is moral or immoral. What is immoral is the treatment of people of color on this island— their relegation to second-class citizenship. In your view, they are only fit to pick cranberries and to clean up after white folks." Ava's eyes were slits of fury and her jaw set.

Superintendent Mitchell attempted to speak again, but Ava held up her hand. "You will let me speak, sir. I will not submit to this witch trial. You will judge me on the merits of my work and that alone. Should you choose otherwise, you will be visited by a lawsuit that may well have *you* picking cranberries," she said, looking directly at Superintendent Mitchell with a satisfied smile. "This meeting is over." She pushed her chair back, jumped up, and left.

Ava was able to hold it together until she reached the dirt parking lot just beyond the school. Once outside, tears streamed down her cheeks. She shivered then suddenly felt flushed. She wiped her eyes as she picked up her pace down Academy Hill. She turned right on Centre Street and followed it down to Main. She had arranged to meet Angie at the park bench on the corner of Orange and Main. She knew she would need to talk to someone after dealing with the schoolboard, and Angie was her dearest friend.

They had been friends since Cyrus Peirce Elementary school. Angie was the only colored girl in her class, ignored by the other girls and boys. There was never any name-calling; they just wouldn't play with her. It was as if she were invisible. They lost touch when Ava went to college, but when she returned, they picked up as if no time had passed.

Angie waved as Ava approached.

"Let's get an ice cream," Ava said playfully, wanting to shake off her foul mood after dealing with the *school police*.

They re-crossed Main Street and headed down to Dunhum's, the drugstore on the corner of Main and Federal with the best ice cream and soda fountain and a great selection of comic books, magazines, and candy.

When they were girls, Angie and Ava loved to sit at the soda fountain and order a "down-the-line" and a package of Nabs each. A "down-the-line" was seltzer water with a squirt of every syrup flavor. This multi-flavored concoction would revolt anyone with a taste for fine food and drink, but Ava and Angie loved it because it was like getting several drinks for the price of one.

The ladies entered the store through the narrow doorway as other customers were exiting. They went directly to the counter and took seats on the shiny, red, round stools.

"Can I help you?" asked the soda jerk, who was clearly an off-islander working there for the summer, most likely a college student.

They looked at each other and laughed as they gazed at the line of syrup dispensers.

"Vanilla cone with sprinkles," said Angie.

"I'll have the same, please," Ava said.

"One or two scoops?"

"Make it two," Ava said impulsively.

Angie nodded.

They paid, and the young man behind the counter handed them cones with extra sprinkles.

Ava took a big bite of her ice cream.

Angie laughed. "You're the only person I've ever known who bites her ice cream."

"I just needed a huge mouthful of sprinkles to get rid of the sour taste from dealing with the three commandants."

"Yeah, no kidding!"

They headed outside to find an empty bench where they could talk.

"Doesn't sound good. How'd it go?" asked Angie, licking the cone as the bottom scoop dripped faster than she could keep up.

"As I expected. They wanted to play the morality card, but I beat them at their own game."

Angie looked at Ava quizzically.

"I told them they were immoral and needed to look to themselves before they judged others."

"How'd that go over?"

"It made no impression, I'm sure. But I'll bet my dad will make a point of running into Superintendent Mitchell on poker night to underscore the message."

"How is your dad dealing with your…" Angie asked, careful not to characterize her situation.

"You know my dad. He's laid back, and for a judge, he doesn't judge people outside the courtroom." Ava paused, reflecting on the situation. "He would prefer that I not be involved with a married man. He's less concerned that Ray is colored, but I'm sure deep in his heart he would like a single, white partner for his only daughter."

Angie reached over and touched Ava's hand, lingering for a moment. Neither noticed Angie's brown skin set against Ava's pale white completion. Even if they had noticed, they wouldn't have cared.

"What about Ray? How's he handling all this?" Angie asked, munching her ice cream cone.

"He's hanging in there. He's taking all the heat, but it was actually Veronica who was playing around first. We met at a parent/teacher event and got to talking, and you know how it goes," she said, smiling. "Talking led to touching, and so on. He's a great guy, smart, a deep thinker, and he worships his kids, who are taking this really hard."

"Where do you see this going?" Angie asked innocently. "Do you love him?"

Ava glanced across the street, then turned to look at Angie. "I like him a lot. I enjoy his company. I'm not prepared to commit to anything more at this point. He's got issues to work out, and I have to figure out what I really want." She paused to lick the melting ice cream off the cone. "Whatever we do will be our decision, not the schoolboard's, my parents', or influenced by Nantucket's cultural norms. That's for damned sure!"

The Pierces had a lovely home on Coffin Street off Upper Main Street. Coffin Street was named after a famous whaling family in

Nantucket. The house was a beautiful two-story structure—very Nantucket-looking with a colonial façade and a widow's walk, a railed rooftop platform with a small enclosed cupola. Widow's walks were built so whaling captains' wives could search for their husbands' returning ships in the harbor. It wasn't a mansion of Monomoy but stately, nonetheless.

They were a close family, just the three of them.

Her parents weren't surprised by the gossip; Ava had already told them about Ray Pereira.

Melvin Pierce, Ava's father, was not happy that his young daughter lived with an older, married man of color, but he knew his daughter well. He brought her up to "live to the truth," as he put it, the truth that we were all equal under God and needed to be treated equally.

"She has learned too well," he told his wife Evelyn, shaking his head, half-smiling.

"Kids nowadays take things too literally," was her only reply.

"Did she have to pick a guy who was married?" he asked rhetorically. He never mentioned the fact that Ray was colored or older. As a father, those things worried him, but he would defend his daughter and her choice, without equivocation.

Mai and Aunt Mabel had been so confident that Ray and Ava would not be able to remain on Nantucket or be able to endure the talking and finger-pointing. Still they had underestimated Ava's commitment to her ideals, and they were totally unaware of Melvin Pierce's convictions or the influence he had.

Melvin Pierce was the Nantucket District Court Judge, appointed by the governor back in 1932. When Ava threatened the schoolboard with a lawsuit, they knew it wasn't an idle threat because of her father.

Everyone who knew Melvin Pierce personally called him "MP," his initials, but it also signified his approach to the law. He had been an officer in the army and brought that discipline, that *military precision*, to his courtroom and his public dealings.

Cape Verdeans didn't know Judge Pierce because they had little contact with the courts. Other than the occasional DWI or domestic dispute that the magistrate handled, they were never before the bench.

Judge Pierce made a point of cornering Superintendent Mitchell at the Friday card game at the American Legion Hall.

The judge approached Robert Mitchell at the bar. "Can I buy you a drink?" he offered.

"Evening, MP. Sure. I'll have a bourbon and water," he said to the bartender.

The judge wasted no time. "I understand that Ava was called in to see you." And he let that drop.

"It's an unfortunate situation..."

"How so?" he baited Mitchell, who took the bait.

"Members of the educational community must be above reproach," he said with stiff posture.

"You mean like David Morse?"

Morse had been caught by the police making out with one of the teachers in his car. Both were married at the time.

It never made the local newspaper, but men gossiped. It made the rounds at the police station and the poker table at the American Legion Hall.

Red-faced and feeling the pressure issued with military precision, Mitchell reached for his drink, knocked back the bourbon, and swallowed hard.

"No reply necessary," said the judge. "My daughter is off-limits. Is that understood?"

Mitchell nodded.

The judge smiled and walked away, calling out to one of his Friday night cronies.

The Pierces were in their own minority on the island—those who believed that the racial policies, many of them unspoken, ran counter to Christian values, equal opportunity, and plain fairness. But they had been silent.

After several poker hands, the judge announced to the table that he wasn't feeling it tonight and was going to make it an early evening. He had been unable to concentrate on the game, his mind preoccupied with his daughter's predicament, its broader implications, and his neutrality. He was not one to stand on the sidelines, but it was unclear what role he could play that would alter the current situation, but his conscience had been awakened.

TEN

....

My FAVORITE THING ABOUT SUMMER WERE THE beach parties, and Dionis Beach was the place to be. It was unclear how the parties came together, but word would magically spread and everyone knew what time to show up and what to bring.

Of all the beach party essentials, beer was number one, followed closely by snack food—chips, pretzels, peanuts, crackers, and marshmallows. Some who were more serious about their food brought charcoal grills, hot dogs, hamburgers, corn, and the associated condiments.

Beach parties were always in the same place. There was a trail that led from the parking lot to the beginning of the dunes which forked off in many directions, all leading to secluded spots.

Following the path to the left led you away from the beach and then turned back, winding just behind the crest of the dunes. At the fourth turn was a large horseshoe-shaped opening that dipped down about ten feet below the crest and then leveled off for another 40 feet before it dropped off again to the water's edge.

It was the perfect location for a bonfire. The cliff shielded us from the wind and offered an endless view up and down the beach and out to sea. Beach parties had been centered in this spot for as long as I could remember and long before that. It was said that if you dug around in the sand you were sure to find buried cans of beer misplaced from previous drunken outings.

The trail behind the dunes continued on for some distance, with many nooks and crannies for couples to claim for their own under the cover of darkness. Once the sun had set on a moonless night a couple could nestle in any one of these areas and have total privacy from onlookers as long as they were quiet with their love making. For the less adventurous couples, ones who did not want to risk exposure, or didn't like sand in their hair, there was always the parking lot. Car and truck windows would steam up, concealing the identity of the lovers inside. The only problem was that everyone knew most of the cars or trucks by sight. So, no one was fooling anyone.

It was Friday, July 3rd, my 18th birthday, but I had said nothing to Lisa about it. I had made a pathetic appeal at work to get the night off. I worked my normal breakfast shift and did extra work to minimize the impact of my absence.

Lisa and I arrived early with Terry and her boyfriend who had come down from New York for the weekend. They planned to make a day of it before the soiree began.

Terry had borrowed her brother's pickup truck. Her boyfriend, Martin, was driving. Lisa and I rode in the back with the beer, blankets, sandwiches, and soft drinks. Martin, who was 22, had purchased the beer for us.

I wasn't much of a beer drinker. I simply didn't like the taste or perhaps it was all alcohol consumption and the deleterious effects I observed that turned me off. But I said nothing and went along with the crowd. I could nurse a beer for an entire night, no problem. But it was only 2:00 pm when we arrived. We claimed the ideal spot, at the head of the horseshoe, laid out our blankets, partially buried the cooler in the sand to slow the melting ice, and stretched out to enjoy the sun.

Leaning back on our elbows facing Nantucket Sound, we could see an occasional sailboat floating by. We could also see the Steamship Authority carrying day trippers back to the mainland.

It was a postcard day, calm winds, clear blue sky, and the white sandy beach stretched for miles in both directions.

Terry coaxed Lisa down to the water, leaving Martin and me up on the bluff.

"I'm sorry, I never got your last name," I said, starting with a neutral topic.

"McBride."

"Is that Scottish?" I asked with a smile.

Martin placed two fingers on his lower arm and rubbed them back and forth, referencing his complexion. Martin was medium brown-skinned. "There are some white folks somewhere in the family tree."

Feeling a little awkward, I changed the subject. "How long are you here for?"

"Just for the weekend. Can't afford to be away any longer," he said, his eyes tracking the girls in the water.

"What kind of work do you do?"

"I'm a courier."

"What does that mean?"

"I pick up money from small businesses and drop off deposits at the bank."

Martin lifted up his trouser leg to reveal a small chrome-plated pistol strapped to his ankle and quickly covered it again. He wore a tough guy expression—squinted eyes and a locked jaw.

I was taken aback. *Who wears a gun to the beach in Nantucket?* I had wondered why Martin wasn't wearing a bathing suit like the rest of us. "Why do you need it here? Are you some kind of beach vigilante?" I said, teasing.

"I have a license to carry," Martin snapped. "I don't like leaving it laying around. Never know who might swipe it."

Clearly, he had a Manhattan mindset and knew nothing about the docile island life. Other than an occasional DWI or domestic dispute, there was no crime on the island, certainly none requiring a firearm.

We sat in silence for a few minutes as I wracked my brain for a topic that might be of interest to him. Finally, I asked, "How long have you known Terry?"

"I met her a few months ago through a mutual friend. It's just a casual thing," he offered. "What's with you and Lisa?"

"What do you mean? We're just friends," I said, downplaying our relationship. *It was none of his business.*

"You know she has a boyfriend back in the city?" he said in a tone clearly designed to set me straight.

I knew not to follow Martin down that rabbit hole, so I quickly asked. "What's New York City like, anyway?"

"How do you mean?" Martin asked.

"You may or may not have noticed but people of color are limited to where they can go and what they can do on the island."

"Yeah, I picked up on that when we were down on Main Street yesterday. The city's a big place. As long as you're in Harlem, East

Harlem, and parts of Brooklyn, you're okay. On a day-to-day basis, the race thing isn't in your face. If you venture into Midtown Manhattan, it's a different story. You'd better bring a friend with you." Martin looked down to his leg with the hidden pistol. "And keep your eyes open."

Lisa waved for me to join her. She was doing cartwheels at the water's edge. I loved her spontaneous vitality. I hoped it would rub off on me and I'd learn to get out of the prison of my mind and live. Just live. As I headed down to the shore, the warm sand between my toes, Terry made her way up the beach.

"How's the water?" I asked, smiling.

"Wet," said Terry with a dour expression.

Her comment struck me like a slap in the face. No matter what I tried she made it difficult. Perhaps I just rubbed her the wrong way or maybe it was something else. I shook my head and scowled.

"What's wrong?" said Lisa, running up to me.

"It's Terry. She's got a vendetta against me."

"No kidding. I can't figure it out." Lisa took my hand and we strolled down the beach. "She keeps asking me what I see in you."

"And what do you say?"

"That I've never felt this way about anyone. Terry says, 'But he's not handsome or manly, and he's a know-it-all who doesn't actually know it all.' And I say, 'He is to me.' She's a good friend but she's getting on my nerves. I wish she would let it go."

I was worried that with her persistence, Terry would eventually get Lisa to see her point of view and she would dump me.

We walked hand-in-hand for a while and came upon a section of the beach with patches of seashells. Lisa picked up and inspected them before tossing them back into the water. Lisa found a conch shell and held it up to her ear. It was beautiful, a lovely pinkish coral inside.

"I don't hear the sea. Do you?" She held it up to my ear, her hand touching my cheek sending a jolt from my face down my neck to my torso.

I listened and heard a whooshing sound. "I hear something, maybe it's the sea. I don't know."

She listened again and then smiled mischievously. "Well, I don't hear the sea, but it told me today's your birthday! And guess what? I just so happen to have a surprise for you later."

"Who told you?"

"Are you saying that shells don't talk?" she remarked with her hands on her hips.

"Not on Nantucket they don't."

"Maybe you don't know how to listen… to shells or girls!" she laughed.

I grabbed her by the waist and threw her over my shoulder like a sack of potatoes. She squealed and feigned outrage by kicking her legs and lightly pounding my back. I carried my precious cargo toward the water. She giggled and squealed so much people were looking our way. Normally I didn't like to cause a scene, but with Lisa I didn't care.

"If you take it back, I won't dunk you," I said.

"Hmm…"

"I'll count to ten and if you haven't taken it back by then, you're going in! Ten, nine, eight, seven, six, five, four, three, two…"

"Kiss me," she said, which if I had thought about it, I'd have realized this was a brilliant tactic. Sexual distraction will get a guy every time.

I put her down and she took my hand, pulling me toward the water. We sprinted through the ankle- and knee-deep water until we were in far enough to float together. We embraced and I kissed her without holding back, without overthinking it, without wondering if she was happy with me as a lover, without thinking one day this might end. Somehow, the water gave me strength and confidence I didn't have on land. She wrapped her legs around my torso and we floated deeper until I could no longer touch bottom. I could've kissed her forever, the water buoying our bodies, pushing us forward and back with the current in a sensual, rhythmic dance. When she was the first to let go, I gasped at her pulling away. I cradled her in my arms like a sodden mermaid as we walked to shore. I loved the feeling of her in my arms, like she was mine and I was hers. And I wished the summer would never end. I dreaded the time life would pry us apart. Cruelly. *Who knew this much happiness was possible?*

I gently lowered her to the sand. I wanted to say, *Lisa I never wanted our kiss to end. I never want this to end*, but instead I said something that took less courage, "Who told you about my birthday, really?"

"Terry. Who else? She told me you wanted your mother to hold out for one more day so you could have been born on the Fourth. Is that true?"

"It is," I said, embarrassed by the admission. "Childhood stupidity. How did she know that?"

"Folklore, I guess," Lisa says jokingly.

Wanting to change the subject from my youthful folly, I said, "Tell me more about the surprise."

"If I did, it wouldn't be a surprise, silly. I want you to wonder." She punctuated the comment by adding, "in anxious anticipation."

I rubbed my hands together to demonstrate my anticipation. Feeling the loss of connection, I took her hand in mine. We continued strolling along the beach when out of the blue, Lisa asked, "What gives with George?"

"What do you mean?" I asked, knowing exactly what she meant. George, Terry's younger brother, was exceptionally light-complexed even for a Cape Verdean. Though this was not unusual, most Cape Verdeans were of mixed race. But George stood out, not only his features, but his hair was almost blonde, something you didn't see.

"He doesn't look like any of the others in his family," she said, giving me a clue as to what she implied.

"Rumor has it, and this was before my time, that Terry's mother, Alice, had an affair and George is a byproduct," I said, lowering my voice even though no one was within earshot.

George was 19, a year older than me but we never played together as children, simply because we lived on opposite sides of town. The gossip back then was that Alice had had a relationship with her boss that led to George's birth nine months later. To call it a relationship would be a misnomer, more appropriately it had been a tryst, a one-time thing.

Alice worked for Norman Layne, who owned a small boarding house that was open year-round. There wasn't much business off-season but Alice would go there each day to make up beds and clean as needed. Perhaps one chilly winter's day they found themselves in one of those rooms.

When George was born, it was apparent to Tony, Alice's husband that the blue-eyed, blonde-haired child was not his. Tony immediately departed for New Bedford never to return. No explanation was given to the children but as time passed and people gossiped, Terry came to understand the reason for her father's absence, but never spoke of it.

When George finally confronted his mother, she told him of her indiscretion.

George loved his mother, he did not judge her, he simply accepted the situation. The townspeople were not so generous. Although Aunt Mabel and Mai did not gossip about Alice, others did.

George was an illegitimate child in a time when labels were used to isolate and discriminate. In a more accepting time and place, this and other delimiting labels have been washed away.

It was probably an hour before we made our way back up to the bluff to join Terry and Martin. Terry was reading a magazine and Martin was staring off into space.

It was around 5:00 pm and everyone was getting hungry, so we decided to pull out the sandwiches that Terry's mother prepared for us.

By the time we finished eating, the day trippers were packing up and leaving the beach. It would be hours before the beach partiers would arrive. Some would come before dusk wanting to set up their private retreat while it was still light, while others would not show up until much later.

The late crowd had only one thing in mind—get drunk and have sex with somebody, anybody.

Beach parties brought together the most eclectic group—young and older teens, young married couples, older married people who would arrive with someone other than their spouse and the occasional single person of any age looking for a hook-up. Spouse swapping was a summer sport on Nantucket Island, a source of entertainment for the participants and fuel for gossip by the spectators. Tonight's beach party would be no exception.

Many folks straggled in by 9:00 pm when the bonfire was a torrent of flames, licking the sky and sending smoke spiraling in whatever direction the wind blew. The singing had begun as the impromptu band, a violin and harmonica player, struck up Cape Verdean tunes. The Cape Verdean's knew the words to every song. Even people who couldn't carry a tune joined in the revelry.

As the night wore on, the crowd thinned. Couples tucked away in the hidden alcoves behind the dunes. Lisa gazed at me in a way that I knew it was time to find our spot.

"Wait, I have something for you." Lisa reached into her beach bag and pulled out a small box wrapped with a bow. "Happy Birthday!"

"Is this my surprise?"

"It's one of them," she said, grinning.

"What can it be?" I shook the box next to my ear to listen to the contents, not that it gave me any more information. I fumbled with the wrapping.

The bonfire had become glowing orange embers, fading into the surrounding night. A waning moon in a cloudless sky allowed me to see. When I opened the box, I was speechless, my heart pounded so hard it felt like it was going to leave my chest. It was a gold pinky ring with a ruby, my birthstone.

Emotions swept over me like a tidal wave. No one had ever done anything like this for me. I tried to speak but words didn't come. It felt so unfamiliar. I usually had an appropriate remark. I reached for Lisa to give her a hug. In my haste, the ring toppled out of my hand. *Damn it!* The sand was a black hole, where things often disappeared forever. There were likely countless treasures buried beneath the shifting sands of Nantucket—a treasure chest full of keepsakes and valuables.

My heart raced even faster than before as we both sifted through the sand in a panic. Over and over, I grasped handfuls of sand and let it sift through my fingers. Nothing but sand and rocks. If it were lost forever, I'd never forgive myself.

Lisa stuck her fingers into the sand, feeling for the ruby ring.

"I'm sorry," I said. "I'm so, so sorry." *Where could it have gone? Was there a sand monster that waited for things to fall and snatched them beneath the surface?*

"Don't worry. We'll find it," she said hopefully.

Her optimism pulled me out of my sinkhole of pessimism.

Suddenly she raised her hand high into the air. "Ah-ha! Found it!"

"Oh, thank God," I said, feeling like such a klutz.

She slid it onto my finger. "I hope you like it."

I grabbed Lisa in a bear hug and kissed her long and passionately. We tumbled onto the beach blanket, kissing, embracing, and gazing into each other's eyes until a partygoer said, "Get a room!"

I sat up, peering at the ring on my finger. "This is the most incredible gift I have ever received. Where did you get it?" I asked, dumbfounded.

"I had Martin pick it up for me. My cousin's a jeweler." She lit up. "Your birthday's not over yet. It's only 11:30!" She smiled, gesturing that it was time to find a place where she could give me the ultimate gift.

I felt aroused just imagining her touch, feeling her lithe body pressing against mine, sensing her depth, and wanting to go deeper. I rolled up our blanket and tucked it under my arm as we set out to find our special spot. I think we must have stayed up half the night. I remember the moon slipping behind clouds, the stars blinking, the chilly dampness of the early morning. I remember sleeping between bursts of passion. I remember it feeling like a dreamscape, like something that would happen to someone else, but in brief moments I knew it was real.

As the first light of sunrise streaked the sky pink, Lisa and I were rolled up in our blanket tucked behind the tall beach grass. I squinted as the sunlight pierced my eyelids forcing them to open. I turned to see Lisa sleeping peacefully, my heart struck by her quiet beauty. I hated to wake her but I had to head to work.

"Lisa," I whispered, "Lisa, wake up. I have to go to work and we need to find a ride to town."

"Wow. You're so lucky," said Anna, her hands crossed in her lap.

"In what way?" No one had ever called him lucky, at least not for the last six decades.

"That you knew such a love," she said, her eyes bright with imagining.

He looked wistfully toward Anna. "Yes, yes, I suppose I am."

"That kind of love only comes once in a lifetime, if it ever comes at all."

"Oh, have you..." Daniel stopped short, realizing it was inappropriate to pry.

Anna nodded but changed the focus back to Daniel. "What happened to her?"

Daniel rubbed his forehead. He suddenly felt very tired, his eyes burned, and his throat was parched.

"Oh, you don't have to answer. It's none of my business, really."

Daniel wanted to tell her but didn't want to burden her with the melancholy yearnings of an old man. He didn't want her to carry the heaviness of life, love cut short. He wanted her to believe that life held promise for a love fulfilled, because his love was just as alive in his heart as it had been in the summer of '42.

"Anna, let's end our session for today. Would that be okay with you?"

"Yes, Danny, I mean Daniel." She giggled and covered her mouth like she had slipped up.

He beamed. "Please, call me Danny. I'd like that very much." It made him feel like the boy he lost long, long ago.

ELEVEN

....

Aɴɴᴀ ᴀʀʀɪᴠᴇᴅ ᴏɴ ᴀ Sᴜɴᴅᴀʏ ᴀꜰᴛᴇʀɴᴏᴏɴ ᴄᴀʀʀʏɪɴɢ a bouquet of flowers.

"Who died?" asked Daniel when she appeared at his door.

"Nobody, silly," Anna chuckled.

"Oh, am I about to die but I just don't know it yet?"

Anna laughed again. "These are for you to enjoy while you're still alive. I thought your room could use a little sprucing up."

Daniel scanned his room and noticed it looked rather dismal. "You mean one framed photograph on a dresser isn't enough?"

"Well, if you're an ascetic, then yes. Here, take a whiff," she said as she held the bouquet up to his nose.

He closed his eyes and deeply inhaled. "Jasmine and rose." He opened his eyes. "Lovely. Thank you. Are you coming from church?"

"Will you think less of me if I say, 'no'?" she said.

"Will you think less of me if I say, 'no'?" he said.

She chuckled.

"The last time I was in church was for my Confirmation. Mai would have been very disappointed if she knew the truth. I had a church deception plan that fooled everyone. Do you think I'll still make it through the Pearly Gates?"

Anna shook her head. "It's not looking good for you." They shared a laugh.

"I just couldn't get past the part where white folks seemed to have a leg up with God. That wasn't a God I could believe in." "Figures the Pearly Gates are white, "Anna said. "It's like a celestial gated community. I might want to go there if the gates were obsidian. But my plan is to become a tree in the afterlife anyway, so I'm not really angling for heaven."

"A tree?"

"Bio urn. It's really cool. Your ashes go into a biodegradable urn and fertilize a tree. Do you know what you want?" she asked, treading lightly.

Daniel shook his head. "Nope, and I don't like to think about it much." He feared death, but not for the usual reasons. If he went to the afterlife without finding Lisa, she might be lost to him for eternity. He was about to ask Anna if she could help him track her down and then he lost his courage.

Anna could clearly see the mood in the room had shifted. "Do you have any stories for me today?"

Daniel's face brightened. "Oh, I have a colorful tale about a Cape Verdean preacher named Papa Godspel."

Her face brightened. "Ooh! That sounds good!" She clapped her hands underneath her chin like a schoolgirl.

Sometimes he caught glimpses of the girl she was and the woman she was becoming.

"But first I must confess…"

It was a Sunday and I was out of the house by 7:00 am while my family slept. I took my usual route, to work, but ended up on the park bench at the corner of Main Street and Federal Street just before church let out. I always timed it perfectly. From that vantage point, I could hear the crescendos and decrescendos of the final hymn. When the parishioners filled with the holy spirit poured out of the church, I'd mix in with them, making sure I was seen. That way, if anyone questioned me, I would have a cover story. But Mai never interrogated me about church, believing I attended early Mass. The rest of my family attended the 9:00 am Mass and then returned home for a late breakfast. Thankfully, no one ever asked me what I thought of the service.

Church was especially important to the women in my family. I really couldn't understand why. I knew if I inquired, they would offer no rational explanation. It was just what they did, what was expected of them, a cultural tradition.

Most Cape Verdeans on Nantucket were Roman Catholic, although in their homeland of Cape Verde their religious preferences were more diverse. Around 70 percent of them were Catholic, two percent Islamic, and another one percent Jewish. The remaining belonged to the pagan religion of Vodun, an ancient religion practiced by some 30 million people of West Africa, with its countless deities, animal sacrifice, spirit possession, and voodoo. This was clearly the genesis of Margaret Santos's beliefs and practices carried on in her home on Washington Street, the ones that had spooked me.

The Cape Verdean women were more devout than the men. I would often find my mother and older sister sitting in the living room in the evening with their rosary beads quietly touching each bead while whispering the Our Fathers and Hail Marys. I sat across the room reading and occasionally stealing glances at them, amazed by the depth of their devotion.

The men, on the other hand, were less interested in religion. While the women attended Mass every Sunday, the men only went on special occasions, Christmas, Easter, Ash Wednesday, All Saints' Day, and maybe the Feast of the Epiphany. Their excuse, a valid one, was that they were working—in winter scalloping and in summer doing lawn maintenance, building, or repairing something.

I was unsettled by the hypocrisy of it all. I wondered, *why were they going to church? To pray to a God that had forsaken them? To tithe money to an institution that looked down on them? To hope for resurrection and a better life?* The way I saw it, the Catholic church was just another anchor placed around the necks of people of color to keep them in their place, at the bottom of the social strata.

The priests treated Cape Verdeans with compassionate disrespect, as if they were children who should know their place and not question why God would want them to be treated as second-class citizens.

As I walked to "church" that Sunday, I noticed flyers plastered all over town on every building and lamppost. Bishop Godspel was coming to Nantucket for a revival meeting. But, as fast as the signs went up, the unseen hand of the town's social police removed them.

The revival would be held on the Pina property, the Barn, out of sight and control of the town selectmen.

The next day when Lisa and I were relaxing on the beach, I said, "We've got to go see Papa Godspel."

"That's a funny name! Who the heck is Papa Godspel?" she asked.

I explained that he was a Cape Verdean ditch digger turned preacher. Born on the island of Fogo, Cape Verde, Domingo Manuel da Papia, he changed his name to Domingo Godspel and adopted the title of Bishop without qualification or credentials.

Daniel leaned forward in his wheelchair. "He was quite the character. Papa Godspel was an early prototype of the modern-day celebrity preacher. He used attention-getting maneuvers such as wearing loudly colored suits with bold, differently-colored piping and shiny buttons, along with glitzy, expensive jewelry and long painted fingernails, all paid for from the contributions of his poor followers."

"Oh, I wish I had been there to see him. If only I could time travel!" said Anna. "Then I could meet your Lisa, too!"

Daniel ignored the comment about Lisa and continued. "For Bishop Godspel and his followers, the miraculous stories as told of the Apostles in the New Testament did not end with their deaths. Papa Godspel, as he was known, asserted that such miracles were once again available through him. He chose 'Papa,' for its papal meaning and not for its fatherly connotation. As Papa Godspel, the bishop and leader of the People's Church, he was well known and respected by his followers as a faith healer and miracle worker, though his works were self-proclaimed and unsubstantiated."

"Despite the legal discrimination of the time, Domingo Papia had found a way to reinvent himself, to shed his poverty and lack of education, to obtain celebrity, and to amass great wealth.

"None of the limitations suffered by Cape Verdeans and Merkanus di kor seemed to afflict Bishop Godspel. He traveled freely in the South, purchased many properties in all-white neighborhoods, and delivered services to mixed-race audiences in the segregated South. This was all possible because of his charisma—that hard to quantify quality.

"Asked by his followers if he were God, he would say no, but he insisted he was his son on Earth, stating God always had one son present on Earth at all times. He inspired hope, a powerful force for the disenfranchised. After all, it was 'The People's Church,' and he made them feel that truth through community activism."

As a boy, I had heard the stories about The Most Holy Papa Godspel and his long, curved fingernails, his fancy dress, and especially his ability to mesmerize a crowd.

Bishop Godspel's entourage arrived on Nantucket ahead of him by steamship—40 or more people, chauffeurs, bodyguards, and assistants, along with three of his fleet of cars, all white Pierce-Arrows. Bishop Godspel refused to suffer through the five-hour boat ride from New Bedford. He would arrive by chartered airplane, directly from Boston, his home base.

A large crowd waited at the airport for Papa Godspel's arrival. In addition to his staff of 40, he brought along another 50 people from the mainland to ensure a crowd of enthusiastic followers were present at the event.

"There it is," someone yelled, as the DC-3 turned on to the final approach to the Nantucket Memorial Airport. It was a beautiful July day with cumulus clouds dotting the sky. There was a slight crosswind causing the DC-3 to sideslip on its approach to the runway.

"The plane is flying sideways," yelled a bystander. But just before the aircraft touched down, the pilot kicked the rudder to straighten it out, a normal maneuver under crosswind conditions. The aircraft taxied to the gate and stopped. The propellers completed their final turn as an attendant wheeled out the movable stairs.

There was a long moment of anticipation before the door opened and another before Papa Godspel appeared in the doorway. A grand entrance was part of the showmanship of a celebrity preacher and he did not disappoint.

He was all decked out in a white suit with wide black cuffs, black piping and a vest, a white fedora with a wide black band, white shoes, and sporting a cane with a gold handle. Numerous braided gold chains with pendants hung from his neck. He was clean-shaven and his hair was long, black, and straight. He looked like a Native American Indian chief dressed in white man's clothes. The only thing missing from the cigar store Indian image was the cigar.

Papa Godspel struck a pose at the top of the gangplank, as if waiting for the press to snap his picture.

He made his way down the stairs and onto the tarmac, walked to one of the Pierce-Arrows where his chauffeur stood with the door open. He placed one foot on the running board and struck a final pose before entering the vehicle. The motorcade exited the airport, led by a state police escort. They were headed for the Barn.

The event was scheduled to start at 5:00 pm and wrap up just before dusk. Bishop Godspel had no plans to overnight on Nantucket. His chartered plane was waiting to whisk him away to Boston. As powerful as he was, he was unable to get any of the white hoteliers to provide him with accommodations.

"Unbelievable. Bishop Godspel was able to overcome so much discrimination but not on Nantucket. So much entrenched prejudice and to what end?" asked Anna.

"Exactly. And the Cape Verdeans who remained, lived on an island of limitations, a world where dreams went to die."

"But you stayed." Anna said. "Why?"

Danny and Lisa didn't go to the airport. Instead they headed for the Barn to beat the crowd. Having become good friends with Sonya, they went straight to her place to wait for things to get started. Not long after they arrived, they heard the commotion outside as the motorcade reached the stage and bandstand. Danny, Lisa, and Sonya peered out the window watching the fuss being made over Papa Godspel.

"This guy is something else," said Sonya, shaking her head. "He came to Philly a few years ago to do one of his revivals. You know why he likes large crowds, besides basking in the adulation? He charges a dollar for everyone he baptizes."

"He won't baptize anyone out here. There's no water," I said.

"Oh, trust me. This guy is creative. He doesn't need a body of water. He's a modern-day Jesus. He uses a fire hose," said Sonya.

Lisa cracked up. "You're kidding—right?"

"Just watch. He'll collect a buck from everyone, talk some shit to the people, and then spray them all with a fire hose."

"Oh, my God! People actually buy into this crap?" asked Lisa.

"He probably has more than a million followers all across the country. So, I'd say yeah. Very much so."

"What brings him to Nantucket, then? He's not going to make more than a hundred bucks if he makes that much," I said.

"Perhaps he knows there are a lot of colored folks here for the summer who can spread his message when they go back to where they came from."

"You're probably right," said Lisa. "I'm sure going to tell every-body I see about this guy."

"But it's probably not the message he wants conveyed," I said.

"You've got that right," Lisa smiled.

Sonya was right. Bishop Godspel was something else. He came out dressed in a black robe, probably because he didn't want to get his fine white clothes wet when he soaked his followers in fire-hose baptism. Who ever heard of such a thing? He was not the char-ismatic, fire-and-brimstone speaker I expected. His diction was poor, his Cape Verdean accent combined with his broken English made his speech stilted and contrived. And true to Sonya's prediction, he collected a dollar from everyone in the crowd before dousing them with a hose that was connected to a pump and a well.

I had never seen such a spectacle. When the water sprayed the women in the crowd, they twisted and contorted like they were possessed. As quickly as Papa Godspel's people stepped in and carried the gyrating women out of the center of the circle, others appeared to take their place. When the baptism was finally done, Bishop Godspel reappeared dressed in his finest to close out the event.

I couldn't help but think of the words of the philosopher, Desiderius Erasmus, who wrote, *In the land of the blind the one-eyed shall be king.* "How blind these people are, not only to this charlatan, but to the many who surround their daily lives," I said just loud enough for Lisa to hear.

"Wow! Such wise words! I sure wish Terry could see you through my eyes." When Lisa kissed my cheek, her lips lingered. I breathed in her sweet earthy scent.

TWELVE

....

Before his sessions with Anna, Daniel had been worried about his memory. When he was a child, his Uncle Joe was placed in Our Island Home with advancing Alzheimer's. Uncle Joe had been an accomplished chess player who played chess by mail. But in his final years he sat in front of a chessboard in the rec-room, wondering what was in front of him. His favorite game had become one more thing he didn't understand. Early on, the staff and his family would load the board with chess pieces, but he would get so frustrated over forgetting what he once knew, he'd hurl the pieces across the room. Occasionally, he'd actually remembered the names of the pieces and yell their names as they ricocheted off the walls. "Damn pawn. God-damned bishop!" He became such a hazard, the staff had to remove the chess pieces and the chessboard sat empty, like his mind.

Because of memory lapses and difficulty finding words, Daniel feared he was headed straight for the empty chessboard phase of life, until he started sharing his stories with Anna. He was pleased to discover his mind was flush with memories; the more he shared them aloud, the more his memories came rushing in.

"The last week of Lisa's vacation went by in a flash. We spent every spare moment together. When I wasn't working or sleeping,

I was with her. Terry was tired of seeing me and didn't hesitate to let me know. But I just ignored her. Sonya, on the other hand, was our guardian angel. She knew Lisa and I had something special. Sometimes when I worked, she and Lisa would do things together."

"Like what?" Anna asked.

"They'd get together and do each other's nails, hair, or makeup. You know, women's stuff. And they would share secrets, like girlfriends do. I don't know what Lisa told Sonya, but Lisa learned so much about Sonya. She was 35, the same age as Tony, her lover in New York, and from Ardmore, a small community west of Philadelphia. She was an only child and her parents divorced when she was young. Her mother had lots of boyfriends traipsing through the house. When Sonya was in her teens those guys started hitting on her. She was raped several times by different guys, but her mother always blamed her. Sonja ran away from home when she was 16, never graduated from high school, and earned her living on the street, using the only asset she had—her body. By 21, she had gotten good at her craft. She told Lisa that she never had a pimp. She said she wasn't going to share the money she worked hard for with no nappy-headed..."

When Daniel stopped short, Anna nodded knowingly.

"Wow. And yet, despite all she had been through, Sonja was such a good friend to you. Without her, where would you and Lisa have been?"

"In the back of a truck, which is what Lisa said she didn't want."

"The world's funny that way. You never know who's going to change your life."

Daniel nodded. "By now my parents had a sense something was going on because I was never around."

One afternoon when I was running out of the house, Mai stopped me in the living room. "Danny, what have you been up to? Where are you going all the time? I hope you're not getting into any trouble," she said, scowling.

"No, nothing like that. I met a girl," I tried to say as nonchalantly as possible.

"What girl?" Mai asked, suspiciously.

"Terry's roommate from New York who's here on vacation."

"Is she Kriolu?"

I knew that was coming.

When I didn't answer, Mai asked, "Is she Merkana di kor?"

I gave Mai a weary look. *I really don't want to have this conversation.*

Seeing my expression, she said, "You know why I'm asking. I'm concerned about you."

"What's that supposed to mean?" I asked, defensively.

"It means that you're too young to know what's best for you," she said with her hands on her hips.

I started to respond when I heard Pai entering through the back door. I knew what was coming next if I said the wrong thing. *N ta da bo un bufatada na boka, I'll slap your face,* Pai's famous threat whenever anyone in our family displeased him. He never actually followed through. The threat was sufficient; no follow-through was required.

I immediately became more obliging. "Her name's Lisa and she's Puerto Rican," I said in an upbeat tone so as to dissuade any further comments about race.

"When are we going to meet her?" asked Mai, her question like a demand.

"She's heading back to New York, so don't worry. I'll probably never see her again." Hearing myself say those words aloud filled me with dread. The thought of not being with her made my heart ache. It gave me courage to request something I had been thinking about. "Pai, can I use, Michael's boat? It's just sitting at the dock. I'll put gas in it and wash it down when I'm finished." I made sure my request covered all potential reasons for refusal. Ironically, I wanted to use Michael's water taxi to take Lisa out to Coatue.

"Yes. But be careful with it. We're trying to sell it."

"Oh, really?" That seemed so sad to me—selling Michael's pride and joy that he worked so hard on. It made me think that when people died, others just sold their dreams. I wished there were something we could do to salvage it.

"You know how to operate it?" asked Pai.

"Yes, I know that Michael put in a standard transmission, clutch and all, so the boat would have enough power for a full load of passengers."

I turned to Mai. "I'll bring Lisa by to meet you... you'll like her."

The next day Lisa packed a picnic lunch and we planned to meet at the Commercial Wharf when I got off work. I bussed the last table and replenished the condiments on all the tables, then made a mad dash down Main Street, bobbing and weaving through the shoppers strolling at a leisurely pace. The sidewalks were packed with pedestrians, so I cut in between one of the parked cars and sped down the cobblestone street running behind the parked cars and vendor's carts.

Once I got to Union Street the pedestrian traffic slowed and I returned to the sidewalk. I turned on to Washington Street and then Commercial, past the ice plant and then it was a clean shot to the wharf.

Lisa was sitting with her back to me, facing the water. I slowed my pace to a walk catching my breath before I arrived. I didn't want to appear over-anxious.

I strolled up behind her, bent down, and kissed her on the neck. "Been waiting long?"

"No, Terry's mom just dropped me off on her way to work."

"Have you been out in a boat before?" I asked, not thinking.

"How do you think I got to Nantucket?" she said, smirking.

"I meant in a small open boat."

"No, should I be concerned?"

"Not with Captain Danny aboard."

We made our way down the wharf and onto the finger pier where Cretcheu was tied up. Cretcheu was the name that Michael gave to his boat to honor his wife.

"What's Cretcheu?" Lisa asked, mispronouncing the name stenciled on the stern.

"Cretcheu (Kreh-T-Cheh-OO) means sweetheart." I corrected her pronunciation. "It was meant for my brother-in-law's wife. He really loved her," I said in a somber tone. I told Lisa the story of Michael and his dashed dreams.

"That's awful," she said, making the sign of the cross. "Maybe someone else could make his dream come true to honor his memory. Maybe you!"

"To be honest, I've never thought about it. The same thing that happened to Michael would happen to any Kriolu who tried to be enterprising. We're supposed to stay in our place—a dead end."

"Oh, I don't know. I have more faith that you could make it happen! You have a quiet strength, a persistence, a keen intelligence that often wins in the end."

I loved that she believed in me, even if the rest of society didn't.

With Lisa's help we cast off the lines and proceeded to the gas pump.

Instead of going directly to Coatue, I decided to give Lisa the grand tour of the harbor. I turned right coming out of the dock and followed the coast line, directing her attention to points of interest as we went. I was in my element as Captain Danny.

When we turned north in the direction of Coatue, the water was a little choppier. I pointed out the mooring in the harbor. "That is where the rich people moor their yachts when they come to Nantucket."

"How do they get to shore?"

"They sink or swim," I said, laughing. "They blast their horns and the launch from the Nantucket Yacht Club comes out to pick them up."

"That must be nice." We smiled at the thought.

"Do you ever imagine you're one of them? I mean, not the haughty or racist part, but the part where the world is your oyster and you have a yacht and a yacht club and people wait on you and life is just grand?"

"Oh, sure. You can't help it living here. It's in your face all the time. I'd love to own a yacht and travel from island to island, always receiving the red-carpet treatment wherever I go. I wonder if it would go to your head."

"Not to yours. You're too level-headed and humble."

We were on the helm's bench seat, huddled together. I held Lisa's hand and occasionally caressed her thigh. "That's Coatue over there," I said, pointing over the port side.

"Where did that name come from?"

"The original people of color on Nantucket."

Lisa gave me a questioning glance.

"The Wampanoag."

"Which Indians didn't have their land stolen by the white man?" Lisa asked, rhetorically.

We shook our heads with a knowing smile.

I pulled up just shy of the beach and dropped anchor. I didn't want to take a chance of going aground or being beached by the tide.

We hopped into the dingy that trailed behind the boat and I rowed us the short distance to shore. We pulled it up on the beach.

"This place is unbelievable—all sky, sea, and sand. And to think we have it to ourselves!" she said, twirling around. "I can see what your brother-in-law was thinking. What an incredible spot... just going to waste," she paused, "until now."

I laid out the blanket. We stripped down to our bathing suits and ran toward the water, holding hands. When we submerged,

Lisa slipped off her one-piece suit and tossed it onto the beach. I did the same, feeling slightly risque but exhilarated.

If paradise exits somewhere, it is right here, today, I thought.

We wrapped our naked bodies around each other, bobbing up and down with the gentle waves, laughing in delight. Lisa dove up and under, flashing me with her bottom. Then she flutter-kicked on her back, her breasts like little islands poking out of the water. Watching her sensual mermaid show drove me to the edge of desire. We stayed in the water until our hands turned to prunes. When we came ashore, we strolled past our bathing suits discarded in the sand.

I tried not to ogle her naked body, but I couldn't help myself. I drank in her perky breasts, her slender legs, her voluptuous buttocks, her wet hair, pink lips, and her green cat eyes. It was all too much to take in. *This beautiful, naked woman is mine for the taking. I must be dreaming.*

We barely made it to the blanket before I pressed her to me. I moved frantically, my hunger for her almost painful. Lisa tried to slow the pace of our lovemaking to help me control my arousal. At one point, she said, "Wait. Danny, please wait. I don't want this to end, not yet."

But I hadn't learned how to pace my desire. I felt embarrassed and wanted to say, *it's just that your beauty, your sensuality carries me away*, but I said nothing. I hoped she wouldn't get impatient with my inexperience and prefer Tony, someone who I imagined would please her all night.

I slid off her and collapsed onto the sand. We lay side by side, holding hands, staring up at the bluebird sky. We were alone in the world, just the two of us, and I wished we could remain that way until the end of time.

"Danny, I'm thinking of staying the summer," she said to the sky.

Motionless, I squeezed her hand. But my insides were singing.

"But I have to go to back to New York for a week to take care of some things."

I hoped those things included ending it with Tony.

Long after Anna left that day Daniel continued musing. There were parts of his story that were just too intimate to share with Anna, but his memories were awaken and he could remember…

It rained occasionally in Nantucket in the summer, like it did the day before Lisa left for New York. When the rain came, people looked for other activities, like puzzles, card games and board-games, and art projects. Some drank the day away. On that chilly rainy afternoon, Lisa and I didn't need to look for an activity because ours was each other. We were at Sonya's place, our secret harbor in the storm. Lisa stood by the window watching the rain dancing on a nearby cottage roof when I approached her from behind. I reached around to unbutton her blouse and undo her bra.

As I caressed her breasts, she arched her back toward me and turned her head to drink in my scent. "Danny, we've known each other for such a short time, but I feel like I've known you all my life. I've never ever felt like this before."

With my hungry hands, I explored her breasts, the silky softness, and the fullness underneath. Before Lisa, I had only imagined what breasts would feel like. The reality was even better. I turned her around to face me. Lisa's areola, so perfect, so symmetrical, so pink, her erect nipples made me weak-kneed. I wanted to take them in my mouth and taste them with my lips, my tongue.

We stayed by the window as I finished the job of undressing her. She willingly accepted my advances, delighting in each moment. The light through the blinds cascaded across her nude torso in ribbons of light and dark. She closed her eyes and threw her head back, surrendering to me, consumed by my touch.

She opened her eyes, green as ocean water, and a smile swept over her face. "I love you, Danny Monteiro. I don't know why but I do." Her voice trailed off as I brought her close for a passionate kiss, magnetic energy flowing between us.

I had no experience with love and had nothing to compare it to. I knew what I felt was powerful, all-consuming. Beyond that I had no explanation, just feelings.

We caressed and kissed our way to the bed in the corner of the room. This would be our last time before Lisa left for New York.

Once again, Lisa urged me to go slowly so we could climax together. She said I'd discover it was like nothing else if I could only pace myself. Her moans quickened as if building toward a satisfying crescendo, but suddenly it was over in a moment of painful ecstasy. I couldn't hold out any longer. I moaned so deeply, it felt like it had come from the center of the Earth.

She sighed in frustration and then showed me how to use my fingers to satisfy her. I could tell it wasn't what she wanted. She turned over and kissed me deeply. "Don't worry. You make me feel something I've never felt before, just your kiss, your touch is enough."

I wasn't sure. It seemed like she was trying to convince herself.

"What are we going to do when summer is over?" she asked.

I paused a long moment, long enough for Lisa's face to drop.

"We can figure that out when the time comes… Love will find a way," I said, quoting an author I had read, hoping Lisa would agree.

Is this what a summer romance is like? I had seen lots of couples hook up for the summer and when the summer was over, so was the relationship. It seemed that people just moved on with their lives, like nothing significant had happened. But that was not how I felt and not how it seemed Lisa felt. *But what could I do?*

"Why don't you come to New York?" she said, her eyes filled with hope.

The thought made me shudder. I didn't want to live in a place where people wore guns underneath their pantlegs. Even worse, what if I had to use the gun in a shootout to protect myself or Lisa? I didn't think I could survive in such a place.

We lay there talking until the sky began to clear and sunlight filled the room. When we heard Sonya in the next room, we decided to get up. I had to get to work and Lisa wanted to thank her for everything. They had grown very close over the past two weeks. How was it possible that it felt like a blip in time but also like an eternity?

I waited outside, dodging the remaining raindrops to give Sonya and Lisa a private moment to say goodbye. Lisa emerged with Sonya trailing her. She had placed her hands on Lisa's shoulders.

"You'd better take good care of this girl or you'll have me to answer to." She gave me a harsh look that morphed into a warm smile.

"Well, with that threat, you know I will!" I said, laughing.

As we strolled to my brother's truck for the ride back to town, Lisa shared her conversation with Sonya.

"She fell in love with a guy who dumped her when he learned she was prostituting herself. She never recovered from that heartbreak. Seeing us in the Barn struck a chord with her. Let's see if I can remember how she put this. It was so beautiful. She said, 'If you could take a picture of love to show others what it looks like, it would be you and Danny staring at each other across that table. You guys have something special. Hold on tight. Don't let it get away. Life is too short. The choices we make, define us.'"

I was startled awake by a knot in the pit of my stomach. This was the day Lisa was leaving. Even though she promised to return, I feared that once back home, she would change her mind, and something, like another man, would make New York look more appealing than the island and me.

I checked the clock: 6:05. I had awakened much earlier around 3:00 am, in a cold sweat. I dreamt that the Steamship Authority ferry taking Lisa to New Bedford had been struck by a torpedo from a German U-boat and that it had sunk, all the passengers lost at sea.

Lisa was thrashing in the water, crying out to me. "Danny, I love you. I'm sorry. I wanted to come back to you," as she slipped under the waves.

"Wait! Wait for me!" I said, but I couldn't move. My legs were frozen.

I sat straight up in my bed, my heart beating wildly in my chest. I couldn't swallow with the feeling of a cotton ball stuck in my throat. I needed a drink of water. My bedroom was on the second floor, at the end of the hall. I stepped out into the pitch-black hallway, not turning on the lights. I knew my way around the house with my eyes closed. The stairway leading down to the first floor was extremely steep. When I was five years old, I fell from midway to the bottom and had a scar on my forehead to show for it.

I gingerly crept down the stairs, straddling the sides of the steps, avoiding the creaking middle. I didn't want to wake my parents whose bedroom was at the bottom of the stairway. I turned the corner at the bottom using the wall as my guide. The door between the hallway and the living room was usually closed, so I felt for the latch. I slid the door open gently to find Pai standing on the other side. I recognized him, but in my half-asleep, half-awake state, my mind did not process what I was seeing quickly enough to stem my blood curling scream.

"What is wrong with you?" Pai asked in a whisper-yell. "I'm not a ghost, at least not yet."

"You scared me. Wasn't expecting..."

Pai cut me off, "Go to bed. What are you doing up anyway?" He went off to bed mumbling under his breath in Kriolu. "Buru, ka teni nau..."

I didn't hear the rest of Pai's rant but I had heard it so many times before. *Stupid, you don't have the sense God gave a mule.* It was Pai's form of tough love.

In the kitchen, I fumbled through the cabinet and pulled down a glass, turned on the tap and let it run for a while, filled it until I felt it running over. I stood at the sink, gazing out the kitchen window. The moon through the clouds cast a faint shadow across the lawn. It was the same light that shone behind Pai, giving him the appearance of an apparition in my half-awake state.

With my thirst quenched, I headed back to my bedroom, carefully opening the hallway door to make sure Pai wasn't waiting for me on the other side.

It took me forever to finally get back to sleep but when I did my nightmares returned.

"What do you think you're doing with my woman?" barked Tony. He was standing in a dark urban alley.

"She's not your woman. You have a wife. Leave me alone. Leave Lisa alone," I demanded but I felt feeble and small, unable to navigate the urban landscape.

Tony lifted his pantleg and I saw a flash of silver.

A pistol!

"She told me she doesn't love you anymore. She's mine, all mine," snarled Tony.

I took off down the deserted street as he fired his pistol. I felt something sharp and hot lodge in my back between my shoulder blades. Before I knew what had happened, my eyes blinked open. I was relieved to be in my bedroom and not in New York City with Tony and his pistol. I figured after that dream I wouldn't go back to sleep. I sat on the edge of my bed for what seemed like an hour but when I looked at the clock, it was only 6:25. I needed to see Lisa right away, maybe to reassure me that my dream was just a nightmare.

She was scheduled to take the 9:00 am boat to New Bedford and we were supposed to meet at the wharf around 8:00 to say goodbye.

I dressed quickly and headed downstairs. When I reached the living room, I heard voices in the kitchen. Pai was usually up and out long before me. He worked from dawn to dusk most every day, no matter the season. Mai, usually slept until about 7:30. What were they doing up together?

"Toma un xikra di café." Mai said to Pai, telling him to have some coffee before he left, when she saw me. "What was all the commotion last night?" she asked.

"I came down to get a glass of water and ran into Pai behind the hall door. Sorry if I woke you."

"That scream could have awakened the dead."

"Sor…ry," I said, stretching it out.

"What's going on with you, anyway?"

"Nothin', I'm off to work. See you later." I scurried out the door, but instead of turning towards Main Street, I went towards Terry's house on Lower Orange Street.

When I arrived, I checked my watch and it was only 7:05 am. I didn't dare knock on the door this early, so I sat on the bottom step. While waiting, my mind raced through all the insecurities mirrored in my dream.

There were German U-boats off the coast of Nantucket. I had read about it in a *Reader's Digest*. The article said, "In May of 1942, the German Navy sent eight submarines to prowl Atlantic waters and destroy ships belonging to their enemies."

What if they attack the ferry? What if it were a fatal blow? What if all the passengers drown? What if I lose Lisa to the sea forever?

Through an open upstairs window, I heard women talking. Listening more closely, I recognized Lisa's and Terry's voices.

"So, I wanted to let you know I'm planning to return to the island for the summer," said Lisa.

"What about your job?" asked Terry.

"I'm going to quit," said Lisa.

"Are you out of your mind, giving up your good job at the law firm for a ridiculous summer fling?"

"Don't worry. I'll continue paying my half of the rent and utilities."

"Where are you getting all your money from? Your sugar daddy?"

"I've been saving money."

"Oh, right. Is that because Tony pays for everything? Is that how you can afford all those nice clothes?"

When Lisa didn't respond, Terry said in a disparaging tone, "You're giving it all up for Danny. What a waste."

Around 7:45, Lisa emerged from the front door carrying her suitcase. "Danny, what are you doing here? I thought we were meeting at the wharf."

"I couldn't wait to see you," I said, racing up the stairs to embrace her.

The mood was broken by Terry's sullen presence. "Let's get going; the Sunday boat is always crowded, everybody trying to get back to the mainland after the weekend," said Terry.

We piled into Terry's mother's car and drove to the wharf in silence. When we arrived, Lisa thanked Terry's mom, grabbed her suitcase, and we crossed the wharf for some privacy. I was holding Lisa's hand, never wanting to let go.

When we got to the opposite pier, Lisa turned to face me. We stood inches apart holding hands and gazing into each other's eyes.

"I'll be back before you know it," Lisa said, trying to assuage my concerns.

No words came, which was unusual for me. This seemed to happen only when I was with Lisa. I tried to turn my forlorn smile into a cheerful one, but Lisa could see the pain on my face and she cradled my cheek in her palm, her eyes filled with love and longing and said, "Oh, Danny, listen... don't worry."

I finally found my voice and the words came easily. "I love you, Lisa. You mean everything to me. I want you to know..." Before I could finish, the steamship whistle sounded indicating the last call to board before the crew pulled the gangplank.

Lisa and I rushed to the gangplank, holding hands as we went. When we reached the gangplank, we shared an embrace and a last kiss. Lisa pulled away when the land-based crew began to untie the gangplank lines.

Seconds later, Lisa appeared on the top-deck railing waving to me and shouting. "I'll see you next week. Have your mother make some canja for me. Love you, Cretcheu!"

I smiled broadly and mouthed, "I love you, too," as the ferry pulled away from the dock. I felt the cleaving apart deep in my bones as though I were the dock and she the ferry.

Lisa and I waved exuberantly as the ferry chugged across the steel-gray ocean, a foamy wake trailing behind. I continued to wave even when I couldn't see her anymore. Stopping would signal our separation.

"Parting is such sweet sorrow," Anna said, quoting Shakespeare's *Romeo and Juliet.*

You don't know the half of it, thought Daniel.

"Did she return as she promised?"

"You'll have to come back another day to find out," Daniel said with a twinkle in his eye. "Isn't it good to end stories with cliff-hangers? Otherwise, you might disappear."

"Oh, Daniel, do you really think that's true?"

He nodded slowly. "Why would a nice young woman like you—when you have better things to do—choose to spend time in this ghastly mausoleum? It's the last stop on the graveyard train. Some here are already walking phantoms, twisted, contorted, bent-over ghouls."

"Are you kidding me? This place is a treasure chest of stories and experiences. So what if the body withers and the mind falters a bit? That's the course of all living things. I'm not put off by the wrinkles. Each line etched in your face is a badge of honor. So much living goes into the furrows and battle scars we carry."

Daniel wanted to jump out of his wheelchair and give Anna a hug for seeing him, rather than peering through or past him, like most people. But since his legs wouldn't carry him to her, he reached out for her, not knowing how he would be received.

She went toward him, leaned over, and embraced him.

When she let go, he said, "Thank you. I needed that." He couldn't remember the last time someone hugged him. In fact, the way he felt, it seemed no one ever had. But it came back to him, as if Anna's embrace had opened up a world he had abandoned long ago, a world too tender to ever return to. He couldn't keep the tears from cascading down his cheeks. "I'm sorry." He wiped them away quickly as if expediency would hide his sorrow.

She offered him a tissue and then stood by Daniel with her hand placed gently on his shoulder. "Please don't apologize. That's how you know you're alive."

THIRTEEN

DANIEL HAD BEEN WATCHING THE RAINDROPS DANCE on the windowsill all morning and the Earl Grey tea he sipped wasn't taking the chill out of his bones. When the cold, soggy, weather moved into Nantucket, nothing took the chill away, except for things that warmed one's heart, like fond memories, good friends, loving gestures. And those were hard to come by when one was tucked away in a place like Our Island Home. When Anna arrived, she noticed he looked cold, and even said his lips looked blue. She arranged his hand-knitted blanket around his shoulders and tucked it in around him. "Better?"

He nodded. "Much."

"Your blanket looks well-loved."

"You can say it—old and worn out, like me." He chuckled. "I can't seem to get rid of it, though." He drew it closer. "My Aunt Mabel made it. She loved to knit and gossip—her two favorite things."

"Oh, stitch and bitch!" Anna said.

"Excuse me?"

"It's a popular activity among women. They stitch, bitch, and gossip about life—husbands, children, money—you name it."

Daniel laughed. "Aunt Mabel was always a woman before her time."

He had been thinking about his mom and Aunt Mabel a lot. He wasn't sure why. They often came to him in dreams and he awoke feeling their presence so strongly, he could swear they were there with him. Maybe as one approached death, one felt closer to those who had already crossed over into the spirit world. Maybe it was a sign. He shivered, not because of the chilly dampness but because he wasn't ready to face the unknown.

"Mai wanted the best for me, but her view of what was best was narrowly defined. As a teen, I found her meddling oppressive, but in hindsight, I know she loved me fiercely and wanted to shield me from hurt, discrimination, and heartbreak. To bring your child up in a world that will treat you as a second-class citizen no matter what you do has got to be troubling. How do you teach your child to have confidence and yet cater to the race that can do them permanent harm—even kill on a whim without worrying about being convicted of murder?"

"Oh, I know," Anna said. "My mama taught me to be a fighter and said although the world would see my color and treat me accordingly, I wasn't to let that define me."

"Did you succeed?"

Anna laughed. "I'm still working on it."

"Well, you seem like a confident young woman to me. So, your mama did a good job."

"She did, although she tried to keep me from falling for a white guy, and it didn't work. I fell head over heels. In the end, she was right—he walked away because he 'couldn't see having children with a brown girl.' His exact words."

"Oh, I'm sorry, Anna."

"No biggie," she said as she waved him away.

But he could tell it was. He could see the hurt in her eyes. He was perceptive like that. He had been studying faces for nearly a century to determine if they meant him harm or good, to determine what was behind the mask everyone wore. "No mother can stop life from scarring her children no matter how hard she tries. I suppose a mother's job is never done, no matter how old her children. Knowing when to let go is probably a tough call.

"I'd love to hear more about your Mai and Aunt Mabel. They sound like characters."

"They were. They certainly were. Oh, and I have a story about Pudgy, the town bookie, also a character. Would you like to hear that one, too?"

"Yes, please!" Anna said, her eyes lighting up.

Aunt Mabel stopped by our place for an afternoon gossip session with Mai. At least two or three times a week, depending upon the juiciness of the gossip, Aunt Mabel parked her 1934 Studebaker *illegally* in front of the house when she visited. The road was simply too narrow for two-way traffic when cars were parked on the side of the road. It actually wasn't illegal per se, but it was certainly discourteous. But that was Aunt Mabel. It was her version of rock-star parking and no one was going to stop her.

"I'm worried about Danny," Mai said, her brow furled. "He seems preoccupied with a girl he's seeing."

"Terry's mother told me that she left last Sunday. But there's more to Alice's story," said Aunt Mabel, her hand busy knitting light-blue baby booties.

Not taking the bait, Mai said, "Danny isn't like my other kids. He has always been different. He has his own way of seeing the world. His head is always stuck in a book. He shows no interest in his father's and brothers' work. He has soft hands and a soft heart. I don't know how he's going to make it in this world," she said, wringing her hands. "And now this."

"Don't worry. Kids find their way. You just have to give him time. You can't live their lives for them. Anyway, Alice said she overheard Terry and the girl..."

"Lisa," Mai asserted. "Her name is Lisa."

"She heard her say that she was coming back for the summer. Alice also told me that she was running around with Cora's husband, in New York."

"Tony Fonseka?" Mai asked incredulously. "Madeline must be beside herself." Madeline was Cora's mother and Mai's close friend.

"I don't think she knows. I don't even think Cora knows."

"How does Alice know?"

"Terry and the girl, Lisa, are roommates in New York. Terry is probably the one who introduced them." Aunt Mabel's needles clicked and clacked.

"Are you going to say anything to Madeline?" asked Mai.

"It's not my place to tell her." Aunt Mabel was a gossip but always cautious with whom she gossiped.

"Si N podi da bo un konsedju... fika kaladu," my advice to you is to say nothing.

When a crucial point needed to be made, Mai would always revert to Kriolu, not that she didn't trust her command of English, but it was just more comfortable. In fact, she was fluent in English and Portuguese. Portuguese was the language of commerce for the Cape Verde Islands and Kriolu was only a spoken language. Since Mai's parents were illiterate, they had Mai study Portuguese in school and asked her to pen their correspondence to family back home.

Though they had no plans to share news with Madeline, they discussed it at length and reveled in the scandal. It made them feel alive to have scandalous secrets. Life as a soap opera.

"How long ago did Tony and Cora get married?" Mai asked.

"Five, six years at most. It was a huge wedding, too."

"Cora was such a beautiful bride and she is still gorgeous."

"What's wrong with men today, anyway?" asked Mai, frowning.

"Oh, you know. It's not just today. Jose was a dog."

Aunt Mabel had divorced her first husband, Jose, after she caught him cheating on her. Mabel wasn't the type to tolerate infidelity or suffer fools.

Ready for a new thread of gossip, Aunt Mabel said, "I saw Ray and Ava Pierce at the A&P shopping like they didn't have a care in the world."

"What a shame for Veronica."

"Well, truth be told, she's no angel. She was going around with some Merkanu di kor all last summer. What goes around comes around, as they say," Aunt Mabel said.

"What do these people think they're doing?"

"Oh, I don't know. Don't you suppose it's cabin fever? After being cooped up all winter with no outlet for frustrations but one another, summer comes and, Aes ta ba dodu," they go crazy. This was another Cape Verdean-ism, the half English, half Kriolu sentence.

"I'd like his father to talk with him but, given that he's a man of few words, I'm going to have to do it myself." Mai said, looking irritated.

"I don't envy you one bit. Well, I'd best take my knitting and head home to cook supper. A woman's work is never done." She carefully set her half-knitted baby booties in her pocketbook, kissed Mai, and disappeared out the front door. If she had been paying attention, she would've seen that cars were backed up in both directions on Washington Street as they attempted to get around her 1934 Studebaker. But, oblivious to the traffic jam she'd caused, Aunt Mabel crossed the road, jumped in, and drove away, waving to Mai on the porch as she went.

Pudgy Pina parked in his usual spot on Main Street, two spaces south of the A&P and directly across from Miss Maple's Sweet Shop. He was there every day between 11:00 am and 3:00 pm, listening to the radio. He preferred catching the ballgame when it was on. Otherwise it was just background noise to pass the time.

His car was basically his office, a brand-new 1942 Chevrolet Master Deluxe, the rare "blackout" edition, so named because it had no chrome or stainless-steel trim, a function of World War II thinking.

Pudgy Pina always had the latest model car. It was his trademark. He was the local bookie, another entrepreneurial endeavor of the Pina clan. I never knew his real name. Everyone called him Pudgy, which he preferred.

Pudgy was in his late twenties and resembled a young Santa Claus with puffy cheeks, a jovial smile, and a roundish body. He was a classic endomorph—high body fat and pear-shaped, with an appetite to match.

Pudgy had inherited the business from his uncle when he passed on. But he was a natural. He was not only a mnemonist, he was also a whiz at math, every bookie's dream. He never wrote anything down for his records. He didn't need to. Pudgy remembered everyone's name and the amount they bet. He gave his customers a small piece of paper the size of a postage stamp with their bet on it. It was their proof. He didn't need any.

I often wondered how Pudgy was able to run his business right on Main Street with people going by, the police walking their beat, and Miss Maple never complaining. Or at least if she did complain, he wasn't asked to move his car. I surmised that Pudgy was paying police protection, an extension of the payments being made to allow the Barn to operate without disruption, which was pure conjecture on my part.

"Danny, when you go uptown, can you play this number for me?" his sister Marie asked.

Marie was hooked on the numbers, combined with her superstitions, she was always having a dream or a premonition that some number was going to come up. She had won enough times to keep coming back, but not enough to have made a profit or beat Pudgy's odds. Marie always boxed her numbers. Her favorite number was 324. Boxing it meant if any combination of 324 came out she would win. The winning number was derived from the para-mutual racing results posted in a Boston daily newspaper.

Bookmaking was illegal gambling but it was a *victimless crime*, so I figured no harm, no foul. Cape Verdeans were betting mostly dimes and quarters, but for Pudgy, it was a lucrative business.

"Danny," Pudgy yelled out as I approached his vehicle.

"Hey, Pudgy. How about those Sox, last night?" We dissected the game for a few minutes.

Marie had another dream last night about 324. "Three-twenty-four and box it," I said.

"Who is that fine young thing I keep seeing you with?" he said, raising his eyebrows a few times.

"Her name's Lisa. She's a friend of Terry's." Everybody knew everyone, so no further explanation was necessary.

"Are you?" Pudgy made an obscene gesture with his hands, simulating intercourse.

None of your business. I just waved him off.

"Seen you two hanging out with Sonya, out at my brother's place." Referencing the Barn. "Steppin' up, huh?"

Not wanting to play Pudgy's game, I said, "Got to cut. I'm going to be late for work." I waved as I hurried away.

As I rushed up Main Street for my second shift at the Pleasant Street Inn, I glanced back at Pudgy and couldn't help but smile. The number of times I'd seen his distinctive Chevrolet parked adjacent to Sonya's cottage was in the dozens. Pudgy made the perfect customer for Sonya, not a lady's man and flush with cash. I was still smiling about Pudgy when I got to the Inn.

"Danny, there are a bunch of tables that need bussing," yelled a young brunette waitress, rushing past me to get her order.

"Okay. I got it!" I shouted back.

"Danny, they need you out front," yelled the desk clerk peering into the kitchen. In Danny's dual role a bellhop and busboy he made several uniform changes a day to ensure he presented the proper image out front or in the kitchen.

When Lisa asked me about my job, I said, "Sometimes I feel like Superman. I'm always in the closet changing." She threw her head back and laughed.

But that day at work, I wasn't my normal efficient self. I was distracted, thinking about Lisa, when or even if she was returning. Usually, I had the tables bused before the patrons had left the dining area. The condiment trays were always full and the place settings and table cloths were always perfectly aligned. One time the restaurant ran out of teabags, and I collected a bunch of them from bused tables and hung them on the clothes line outside to dry so the waitresses could reuse them. We all had gotten a good laugh out of that one.

But that day, people had to keep prompting me to do things that I normally did without being asked. I even dropped a tray full of dishes and glasses in the dining area, frightening customers and creating a huge mess of shattered glass and porcelain for me to clean up. One of the waitresses stopped by the mess I had created, placed her hand on my arm, and asked, "Are you okay? You don't seem like yourself today."

"Yes, yes, I'm fine," I said, covering up. I just wanted to get out of there as quickly as possible before I did any more damage.

When I finished my shift, I headed down Main Street, my feet like molasses but my mind racing. *What is Lisa doing right now? Is she thinking of me as much as I'm thinking of her? Does she miss me?* I knew the last question was ridiculous because she had just left yesterday. But to me it seemed like she had been gone a week, a month even.

I spotted Terry's mother's car coming up Main Street. I stepped out onto the cobblestone street in between two parked cars and waved her down. She slowed to a stop.

"Have you heard from Terry?" I asked.

"Yes, she called last night to say that they arrived home safely."

"Did she say anything else?"

"Oh, Danny, gotta go! I'm holding up traffic."

I acknowledged her with a wave. I knew that the call would not have been a conversation. Long distance calls were very expensive, so poor people had devised a way to call collect and leave a coded message. The way you let a loved one know you arrived safely was to call collect asking for a fictitious name. The party on the receiving end could hear you talking to the operator and they simply did not accept the charges.

When I got to Union Street, I decided to go home the back way. I was in no mood to have Aunt Mabel tap me for one of her endless chores. It wasn't that much out of the way. I followed Union to Lafayette. Our house was on the corner of Lafayette and Washington. I tiptoed in so as not to be noticed, but our creaky front door gave me away every time.

"Danny, is that you?" Mai called out from the kitchen where she was clanging pots and pans.

Oh, brother. Here it comes. By the time I made it through the hallway Mai was in the living room, potholder in hand, looking stern. "We need to talk."

I sighed dramatically. "Mai, I'm tired. Just got off my shift. Can we talk later?"

Mai said, "Xinta," which meant sit.

I knew by her tone the answer was 'no.' So I reluctantly sat on the couch, but with one leg extended ready to bolt the minute I could.

"We need to talk about your girlfriend, Lisa."

"What about her?" I asked, defensively, not making eye contact.

"How come you didn't tell me she was coming back for the summer?"

"You didn't ask."

"Don't get fresh with me. What's going on between you two?"

"What do you mean, 'what's going on?' We like each other and spend time together, like most people our age."

"Do you know she's having an affair with a married man?"

I refused to take the bait. I let her continue before saying anything. Mai was primed after her conversation with Aunt Mabel.

"What kind of girl goes out with a married man? I'll tell you what kind—a hussy!" Mai exclaimed.

"Where did you hear that?" I knew about Lisa and Tony Fonseka but I didn't know it was public knowledge.

"Your Aunt Mabel told me that Terry told Alice…"

"I should have known. It's the ol' gossip network. Gotta hand it to you. You're better than the FBI," I said, sarcastically.

"Kuidadu," careful, Mai said, shooting me a cautionary look.

I knew what that meant. Any more disrespect and she'd whip out the infamous, bufatadu na boka, slap-across-the-face admonishment.

Although I was angry, I knew how to tread lightly. I wanted to say, *Aunt Mabel is a nosey busybody*, but I thought better of it. I took another tack.

"Why is Lisa the villain? What about Tony Fonseka? He's the one who's married. He's the one who exchanged vows in church. Why does he get a pass?" When Mai didn't respond to my rhetorical questions, I continued. "He's the one who made the commitment. Lisa has no obligation to Cora. She doesn't even know her." It wasn't true but I threw it in for good measure. "Anyway, she's not seeing him anymore." Seeing that Mai was losing her conviction, I fired one more volley. "You don't even know Lisa and you're already passing judgment on her."

"She is obviously experienced and you're still just a boy. Women mature way faster than men..." She hesitated, clearly uncomfortable finishing her thought.

I realized she had a valid point. Lisa was way more experienced in the area of romantic relationships, but, despite that, I felt we were intellectual peers. "Mai, I want you to reserve your judgment of Lisa until you've had a chance to get to know her."

It surprised me Mai hadn't mentioned that Lisa was Puerto Rican and not Cape Verdean. *Cape Verdeans are just as prejudiced and narrow-minded as any white folks, but they don't see it that way. People never do.*

I hightailed it out of the living room the minute I saw an opening. I had performed my duties as a son—fielded all my mother's prying questions. I felt impatient with her and anyone who questioned our private, passionate love. It just didn't seem appropriate for something so sacred to be subject to the glare of a blinding spotlight.

The remainder of the week passed at a snail's pace. I did all my usual things, lived my life the way I did before Lisa, but it was all wrong. Things that used to feel right didn't anymore. It was as if love opened my eyes to what was possible and made the mundane intolerable.

In the daytime, I went to work, came home, and sat out back or in the living room reading to escape. I avoided the beach because I didn't want anyone grilling me with, "Where's Lisa?" "What happened to Lisa?" "Is she coming back?" Because, truth be told, I sometimes doubted it myself.

Evenings weren't any better, and in fact they were much worse. Sleep wouldn't come as it always had. Before Lisa, I would hit the pillow and be out in seconds. But now bed was a torture chamber in which I was plagued by fears about Lisa forsaking me and worries about Tony Fonseka urging her to stay in New York, or Terry and Tony ganging up on her and convincing her not to return. I was in a foul mood, with no appetite and very little interest in anything. I guess you could say I was lovesick.

FOURTEEN

··

THE STEAMSHIP AUTHORITY STEAMER, THE NANTUCKET, was coming around Brant point at 4:49 pm. The steamer was due to dock at 5:00 and it was right on time.

I had parked there and walked out onto the rocks as far as I could go, hoping to get a glimpse of Lisa. People waved at me but I couldn't spot anyone who looked like her. I waited until the vessel had completely passed and made a mad dash for my brother's truck. I wanted to be there when Lisa stepped ashore. I parked in the only space I could find on the far side of the dock.

Taxis, tour buses, minibuses from the luxury hotels, and others coming to pick up family and friends had filled all the spaces close to the terminal. As I sprinted across the parking lot, I could see the smoke stack of The Nantucket, as it backed up into position. I reached the gangplank to find it even more crowded than the parking lot. I stood three-deep in the crowd craning my neck to catch a glimpse of her.

Of course, I had no idea what she might be wearing and I was concerned I might have forgotten what she looked like in the week we'd been apart. But not really. I thought about her every second of every day since we had parted.

My heart skipped a beat when the line of passengers first thinned out and then stopped. But then a passenger in a wheelchair who had been blocking the way appeared and the line was moving again, but still no sight of Lisa. My fears were renewed. *She's not on the boat. Tony convinced her not to come.* Why hadn't I heard something from her? As my mood spiraled into the depths of depression and I played out all the worst-case scenarios in my mind, Lisa appeared, jumping up and down, waving and yelling, "Danny, Danny!"

My recovery was instantaneous. My lungs inflated, my heart palpitated, joy filled my eyes, and I couldn't stop smiling.

By now the crowd surrounding the gangplank had all but disappeared. Just a few stragglers remained.

I rushed up the gangplank moving against the few remaining passengers. We collided. I lifted her and spun her around. She pressed against my body as she slid down to the ground, kissing all the while.

People were showing their displeasure with throat-clearing and a loud, "Excuse me," in having to go around us on the narrow gangplank, but we were oblivious, caught up in our own private world, until a member of the docking crew politely asked us to clear the way.

I made my apologies to him and the passengers, as Lisa and I, now arm in arm headed for the luggage cart.

I didn't know that Lisa had been standing up in the bow area so she could see where the ship was going. She had seen me on the rocks at Brant Point and waved frantically but I never saw her. The gangplank was located at the stern of the vessel, so she was one of the last to disembark.

I wanted to say, *I didn't see you and was so nervous you weren't coming but now that you're here all is right with the world.* But I refrained. I didn't want to seem like a Nervous Nelly. *Play it cool,* I told myself. *Play it cool.*

"Did you bring a lot of stuff?"

"No," she smiled, "Just myself. Isn't that enough?"

For a minute, I thought she was serious.

Her pearls of laughter rose above the din at the port. "Actually, a few shorts, tops, sneakers, and underwear."

"Bathing suit?" I asked.

"No, I thought we would be swimming nude."

That was a dumb question. Okay, no more dumb questions.

Lisa had arranged with Sonya to stay in her cottage. We couldn't wait to get there, but I had to work and was already running late. My second shift started at 5:00, but the tables wouldn't need bussing for at least 45 minutes after dinner started. And I had set up all the tables before I left at noon.

Lisa glanced up from the luggage cart to see Sonya standing with her arms extended. Lisa shrieked her name and rushed over for a big hug.

"Sonya, will you take Lisa home?"

"Of course!"

"I've gotta run. See you at 9:00 tonight." I wanted to kiss Lisa but didn't want to have an audience, so I just took off. When I reached the Pleasant Street Inn, I became a whirling dervish whipping through the dining room, clearing and resetting tables, refilling water glasses, and cleaning up and sweeping. I was hovering above the ground, floating in mid-air. My old self had returned. *Thank God.*

It was 9:14 when I arrived at Lisa's place. She had rented one of Sonya's rooms. She would be living in a brothel for the summer. *Boy, that's going to go over great with Mai.*

Lisa pulled me toward the bed and took charge of our love making. She had taught me not to rush to intercourse but to take my time with foreplay, pleasuring her while she pleasured me. She was a kind and gentle teacher, showing me how to manage my intense libido, my tumescence, and how to return to arousal. A second orgasm was something I didn't even know was possible—for both of us. Before then, my arousal had always overwhelmed me. That night, I learned to unveil our lovemaking slowly, like savoring a piece of candy instead of ripping off the wrapper and scarfing it down.

Exhausted and sated, we fell asleep in each other's arms. Lisa was doubly tired having risen before dawn to catch the bus for a five-hour ride that would take her to New Bedford for a five-hour boat ride to Nantucket.

I didn't wake at my usual hour. Had Sonya not tapped on the door, I would have been late for work again, but I managed to make it on time.

When my shift was over, I headed for home. I knew Mai would not be pleased, so I braced myself for what was to come. The minute I walked in the door, I heard, "Danny, is that you?" from the kitchen.

"Yes, Mai, it's me."

She stood in the middle of the living room with her hands on her hips. "You didn't come home last night and you didn't tell anybody you were staying out. You don't live alone you know. People worry about you. I mean, you could've been dead and we would never have known. Where in God's name were you?"

There it is. What's the right answer that's going to keep the peace? Certainly not the brothel. I'm just going to tell her the truth and deal with it. But before I could answer, Marie popped into the kitchen, having just returned from her job as a chamber maid at one of the small inns on Beach Road.

"Hi, Mai... Danny, haven't seen you around much. What have you been up to?"

"Workin' and hangin' out. You know, summer stuff. How are you doing?" It hadn't been that long since her husband died. I figured she was still heavy with grief.

"I miss Michael so much and Michael junior is a handful. He misses his dad something crazy and is acting out."

Mai interrupted to let Marie know about her displeasure with my conduct. "Danny has a girlfriend."

"Good for you!" Marie smiled broadly at me.

But Mai was intent on poisoning the good mood. "And he stayed out with her all last night. Never came home. Never told anyone."

"Mai, he's grown. Let him have his fun. Life is far too short to sweat the small stuff."

Mai could see that she was being double-teamed but she was determined to stand her ground. She turned to me. "As long as you're living in my house, you will live by my rules. Understand?"

I nodded. I was smart enough not to say anything else. Going forward, I vowed to tell Mai what I was doing. I also planned to bring Lisa by to meet her. I was hopeful that Lisa could win Mai over. Lisa and I had already talked about it and she was all in.

"I know how to deal with mothers," she had said.

I hoped so but I wasn't so sure. She had never met Mai.

FIFTEEN

"WELL, WE HAD A LITTLE EXCITEMENT HERE LAST night," Daniel said, biting one of the gingersnap cookies that Anna had brought for them to enjoy during their session. "Mm-mmm!" He held it up in approval.

"Oh?"

"My sister paid me a visit in the middle of the night—naked!"

"Wait! What? You have a sister here?"

Daniel threw his head back and laughed heartily. "No. That's just it. My sisters left Nantucket years ago. Marie went to Rhode Island and Eugenia to California."

"A woman claiming to be your sister..."

"Climbed into my bed. Boy, was I surprised when I woke up and realized what was happening!"

"You have a more exciting life than me. That's for sure!"

"If you want that kind of excitement."

"What did you do?"

"I didn't want to press my call button and get her into any kind of trouble, but, you know, my legs don't work too well. So, I did ring the on-call nurse and she wrapped Mrs. Griffith in a blanket and escorted her back to her room."

"Obviously, she has some cognitive decline..."

"Or some wishful thinking."

"Okay, but I'm going to state the obvious. What adult jumps into bed naked with their brother?"

"You'd be surprised. May I have another gingersnap, please?"

"Of course. Eat all of them if you want!"

"But what about my girlish figure?" Daniel said in a high voice. "That's what Mai used to say. I didn't have the heart to tell her that her girlish figure was long gone." With ginger and sugar on his palate and cookies in his belly, Daniel was anxious to go back to the time his senses were more alive, he felt vigorous, and life still had plenty of pizazz.

Looking back, the summer of '42 was a delightful blur, bussing dishes and rushing around the restaurant punctuated by hours swimming, romping, and roaming, making love, and sleeping at Sonya's. Moments of pleasure were bracketed by long conversations and dreaming of the future. But in August, I always felt a certain heaviness, with the countdown to Labor Day, the beginning of school, and the prospect of winter. August that year was poignant for me—it signaled the last month Lisa would be on the island.

We squeezed all we could out of the remaining days, which were noticeably shorter and foggier. Each evening, the low-lying fog crept in on cat's feet as the fading sun prompted the warm air to condense into a mist, thick and enduring. The fog lingered until the sun burned it off. Some days it could last well into the late morning.

I had brought Lisa by to meet Mai shortly after Lisa returned to the island. She shared with Mai the story of her growing up, how her family migrated from Puerto Rico to New York, the struggles her parents had assimilating into the city with English as a second language.

Mai saw the parallels between her parents' experiences and Lisa's. She could see how they were not so different; in fact, their cultures were very much alike. But Mai wouldn't be won over so easily, not before she knew Lisa's intentions when it came to me. "So, are you and Danny..." She struggled to finish her question as if she wanted to inquire but was too polite to delve.

Lisa came to the rescue. "Mrs. Monteiro, I love your son. He is such a unique, precious person. I have never met anyone like him in all my life."

Mai could see the light in Lisa's eyes, when she spoke of me. "I remember, oh, so long ago, how I fell head over heels for Manel. Sometimes I felt so smitten, I could hardly speak around him. Of course, now I see him and think, 'Oh, no, you again?'"

Lisa chuckled. "I can't imagine ever feeling that way about Danny."

"Oh, just you wait!" And then Mai realized what she had implied and covered her mouth in a can't-take-it-back moment.

Lisa regularly stopped by for chats, waiting for me to return from work. It became a routine and Mai looked forward to her visits. Some afternoons they would talk long after I returned from work.

On one occasion, Mai shared with Lisa her concerns about my future.

"I don't know how he's going to earn a living. He's not cut out for the type of work his father and his brothers do."

"Danny loves to write," Lisa said with a lilt in her voice and light in her eyes.

"You can't put food on the table by writing," Mai grumbled.

"Some writers earn a living writing stories for magazines or publishing novels. Or even going into journalism."

"They're all longshots. Meanwhile, you're in the poorhouse with no way to support a family or put food on the table. Then your family has to bail you out. It just seems like a fool's playground to me."

"But there are those who break through and I think Danny has promise."

"How do you know? Have you seen anything he's written?"

Lisa smiled and nodded. "The poems he has written for me are lovely."

"He writes poetry?" Mai seemed intrigued, at least for a minute, but said, "Well, love poems aren't going to put a roof over your head."

Realizing the conversation was like a grounded ship strewn against the rocks, Lisa let it go.

Lisa and I had talked about my writing aspirations, mostly at sunset or underneath the stars when one's dreams sprout wings, soar, and have no limits. I loved the feeling of riding the wings of my dreams. And with Lisa at my side, anything felt possible.

Despite my earlier apprehensions about New York City, I decided it could be an incredible adventure, especially with Lisa. She had a way of making everything enchanted, magical, of turning a dreary day into the best day of my life just by being Lisa. There was an alchemy to her presence, as if she changed the way molecules moved, the way the wind blew, the way the seasons shifted. She turned my world upside down. Or maybe it was just me she was changing.

I was willing to go to New York in the fall to try my hand at writing. Perhaps I'd take some courses at City College. Maybe I'd be the next Langston Hughes. I was nervous to share my decision with Mai and Pai. They'd tell me that dreams like that were for rich white kids with a safety net who had the luxury of pursuing flights of fancy, whose mommies and daddies could finance their hobbies. But I wasn't like the rest of my family. I knew there was something waiting for me that was beyond laboring, beyond this insular island, beyond the limitations our people set for each other. It wasn't that I was better than them. I was just not cut from the same cloth. I dreamt of a life they couldn't even conceive of.

Lisa had also met Pai, Marie, Joseph, Freddie, and my younger sister Eugenia. She had a way of winning people over, though Pai was not ready to accept that I was old enough to be involved with such a mature young woman.

When Pai and Mai talked about us, Pai said to just wait until Labor Day, implying that with the change in seasons came a change in minds. He had seen it enough times in his sixty years.

Mai took his comment in stride. She knew he was neither an optimist nor a pessimist but a realist. He accepted life on its terms. When anyone complained to him, he would tell them, "sufri kaladu," suffer in silence.

One Friday night, Lisa was invited over to our place by Mai and Pai when I was working. The next day Lisa told me the whole story.

Everyone was there except for Freddie, who never ate with the family. He always took his food to the back cottage and ate alone. He had been reclusive ever since being discharged from the Coast Guard. Something happened but he just wouldn't talk about it.

"You're pretty," Michael Jr. said to Lisa. He couldn't stop staring at her.

"Thank you and you're a handsome young man," she said, smiling.

"How come you like my Uncle Danny?" he asked, chewing while talking.

"Michael, you don't ask people those kinds of questions," Marie said, tapping him on the shoulder. "And you should wait until you're finished chewing before you talk."

"I heard you ask Mai that," he said, not understanding that he should keep that information on the down-low. Michael called his grandmother Mai because everyone else did. And no one corrected him.

Marie blushed and apologized for Michael. She tried to explain the context of her conversation to Lisa.

"Don't worry about it," Lisa said. I've heard that comment a lot."

Lisa leaned toward Michael Jr. and whispered, like it was their secret. "Because your Uncle Danny is a very special person."

Michael Jr. seemed tickled that she would share such a secret with him. "Ohhh," and he blushed.

"Michael, eat your dinner and don't bother Lisa," said Marie.

Michael Jr. who was smiling flirtatiously at Lisa, turned, and stared at his dinner, pushing the peas around his plate.

"Oh, it's okay. I don't mind," said Lisa. "I think he's sweet."

Wanting to shift the conversation, Marie asked, "Lisa, what do you do for work?"

"I'm a legal secretary for a Manhattan law firm," she said as she buttered her bread.

"What's that like?" Marie asked.

"It's very interesting. I do lots of courtroom transcription. The lawyers don't like to wait for the court stenographer's official transcript, so they use me to record the testimony. This allows them to review it as soon as they return to the office."

"So, how were you able to get the summer off?" Marie probed, taking a sip of water.

"That's just it. I'm pretty good at what I do and my boss appreciates my work, so, when I told him I was going to need some personal time off, he said okay."

"What about your family?" Marie was giving Lisa the third-degree, asking all the questions Mai would have liked to ask but didn't know how to broach. Lisa appeared happy to field Marie's questions.

After dinner Lisa and Marie continued chatting. It was Lisa's turn to ask the questions. She took the opportunity to learn more about me.

"Oh, Danny's a bookworm," Marie said. "He's always buried in a book and then feels compelled to tell us about what he's reading. Sometimes the topics go right over my head but I pretend to be interested. This happened especially when he was younger. Not as much anymore."

Marie looked up when she heard the distinctive creak of the front door. The Monteiros never fixed the creak because it signaled to Mai when her kids were home and she could finally go to sleep.

"Danny, look who's here!" Marie said.

Lisa jumped up and met me in the hallway. She was careful not to be too demonstrative in front of my family. "How was work?"

"Oh, same stuff, different day." I smiled. "But I was attacked by a bat when I went out back to empty the trash. It dove right at me."

Everyone laughed.

"You're kidding, right?" said Lisa.

"I think it was a vampire bat because it went for my neck."

They laughed again, not knowing if it was true or not but enjoying the story, nonetheless.

"Stories don't have to be true to be enjoyed," Daniel said.

"Wait just a second. Are you telling me your stories aren't true?" Anna asked.

Daniel's eyes twinkled. "Are you entertained?"

She nodded. "Of course."

"Then does it matter?"

"They carry more weight if they're true."

"Why? How do you know, for example, we're not just inside someone's imagination? How do you know we're not made up?"

"You know for an old guy, you're pretty darned cool."

"And for a youngster, you possess depth beyond your years."

"You know what? I wish I had known Danny. I think he might've been a good friend."

"You do know him. He has just been aged to perfection. A little like cheese, stinky but delicious."

Anna and Daniel shared a long, hearty laugh.

August brought the carnival to town. A caravan of trucks carting carnival rides floated over on the Nantucket ferry and was deposited on shore. The carnies would head for the Fairgrounds and set up their Ferris wheels for the more daring and merry-go-rounds for the kids. Along with the rides came the carnies and the carnival booths. The carnies festively distracted carnival-goers. Their sole purpose was separating them from their money. They offered ring tossing, dart throwing, and other games rigged to ensure those who ventured their hard-earned money would lose it. And, in the off chance that they did win, worthless prizes were awarded. One spent ten dollars to win a prize worth 25 cents.

Even though the rides were kid stuff and the games of chance were a euphemism for theft, everyone under fifty was drawn to the flashing, twirling, spinning, raucous affair with the sweet scent of cotton candy and pastries wafting in the air.

We planned to go one night after work. I didn't want to drive to the fairgrounds because parking was going to be a hassle. "Let's walk up town and take the shuttle to the fair."

We walked hand-in-hand up Washington Street. The fog thickened as it rolled in off the harbor.

"Is it always this foggy here in August?"

"Yes." I launched into a detailed explanation of physics of fog on our island.

"A simple 'yes' would have been enough," she said as she affectionately nudged me off the sidewalk and into the street.

I pretended to almost fall over and she ran and grabbed me around the waist. We laughed and walked arm-in-arm to catch the bus. When we arrived, the normally empty field was illuminated and flashing. The fog gave the light an eerie glow as it absorbed and diffused the carnival's rainbow of colors. Children's shrieks of glee punctuated the air.

We checked out the booths and rides to see what we might want to try. I bought Lisa a giant serving of cotton candy. We took turns tearing off fluffy pink pieces and popping them into each other's mouths. I loved how the sweet fluffiness melted on my tongue and turned it pink.

Our first ride was the teacup. We jumped into our cup and laughed as we spun one way and then the other, a thrilling dizzying sensation. Next, we rode the Ferris wheel, my favorite since there was no rollercoaster. I loved the feeling of my stomach lurching as the Ferris wheel spun down and up again. We held hands while taking in the bird's-eye view of the carnival and the town clock that glimmered faintly in the distance. After the Ferris wheel, we strolled by the merry-go-round, which I figured we'd skip. Not even Michael Jr. would ride it. He said merry-go-rounds were for babies.

But Lisa pulled me toward it. "I used to love riding this with my dad as a kid."

That was good enough reason for me. I didn't care that we might look ridiculous astride painted horses bobbing up and down with no child in sight. With Lisa, I ceased caring what others might think. She chose a yellow one and I chose the blue one next to hers. I watched her as we bobbed on our horses, and the joy in her face made my heart sing.

We dismounted the slippery horses and strolled through the booths. As we passed one, I spotted a giant teddy bear. "Look at the size of that thing!" I said, pointing at the bear sitting up on the top shelf. In an instant I decided I wanted to buy it for Lisa. "How much is that teddy bear?" I asked the concessionaire.

He was a portly man who appeared to be at least sixty. He looked like he had been working this circuit one too many years and needed to be put out to pasture. But when he chuckled, he seemed jolly. "You can't buy it. You have to win it," he said, winking. The concessionaire explained that if I knocked any of the three sets of three bottle-like objects off the pedestal, I'd have my pick of anything on the top shelf which included the extra-large teddy bear.

"I can do this," I said, glancing at Lisa.

I handed the concessionaire a dollar. He placed three balls on the counter. "Good luck!"

On my first attempt, I knocked one of the bottles off the stand.

"I didn't know you were left-handed!" exclaimed Lisa.

"Oh, that's a long story." I smiled.

I was on my fifth attempt to knock the three bottles off the stand, but each time one or two fell off or tipped over with one left standing, like it was glued or magnetized to the stand.

By my seventh attempt, a crowd had started to gather around the booth. By the ninth, it had grown in size, strangers silently cheering me on.

"You can do this," Lisa said.

I let the next ball fly. It hit the third bottle at its base causing it to slide to the edge, but it did not fall.

On the tenth attempt, my first ball blasted two of the bottles off the stand. The second ball breezed by missing the third bottle by a hair. That shook my confidence for a moment.

Then tapping into my pitching skills that I had mastered when I played peewee baseball, I stepped back from the booth to give myself more room to deliver my final ball, with all the force I could muster. I wound up and let it fly with everything I had. It hit the last standing bottle square on the neck. The bottle wavered and fell forward on the stand, defying all laws of physics.

Boos rang out from the crowd. People waved their hands at the concessionaire in gestures of disapproval. One guy shouted, "These games are rigged," and he stormed off in disgust.

The concessionaire was unfazed, like he had heard it all before. As he reached down to pick up the fallen bottles, I vaulted over the counter and plucked the teddy bear from the top shelf and was out of the booth before the man realized what happened.

"Hey, give that back!" he yelled.

"Not only did I win it, I also paid for it. It's mine. If you want it, come and get it."

The dispersing crowd heard the altercation and stopped to see how it was going to play out. Perhaps they were hoping for a brawl.

The old man could see he was clearly outmatched. He was hesitant to leave his booth empty with the angry crowd hanging around, so he decided to cut his losses. "Get out of here you..."

"Don't say something you're going to regret." I grabbed Lisa by the hand and quickly led her away from the booth. After we had put some distance between us and the concessionaire and I was certain no one was coming for me, I turned to Lisa. "This is for you." I handed her the giant teddy bear with a self-satisfied grin. "When I saw him, I vowed to get him for you no matter what it took."

Lisa took the oversized bear and gave him a squeeze, nuzzling her head into its giant belly. "Oh, I'll cherish him forever. I'll call him Beau, a nickname for my beautiful Danny."

I leaned over and kissed her. *Could I love her any more? Could I love anyone else this much?*

As we strolled toward the exit, I said, "That's enough excitement for one night. Don't you think?"

"My hero," Lisa said, swooning. When we got a little further, Lisa asked, "So what's the long story about being left-handed?"

"Hey, you remembered!"

"Of course, I did, silly."

"Some Cape Verdeans believe that being left-handed is a sign of the devil. It probably comes from some weird voodoo religion in the old country. When I was a kid, Marie would grab my fork out of my left hand and tell me to eat with my right hand until I became accustomed to it. I did everything right-handed, but when I went out for peewee baseball, no one forced me to switch hands, so I threw the ball with my left hand."

"A devilish pitcher!" Lisa said. We chuckled. "It's so funny. Puerto Ricans have the same superstition except they believe that lefties can't get into heaven."

"Well, it was a blessing in disguise, because now I'm ambidextrous."

"I've noticed," she said, flirtatiously.

I blushed and pulled her close. We shared a long luscious kiss that made me want more, but we were a long way from Sonya's.

As the shuttle bus pulled up and we were about to board, we heard a loud resounding boom. The earth literally shook. It was like nothing I had ever heard before.

"What in the world was that?" asked Lisa.

I shrugged. I couldn't even venture a guess. "Don't know but it sounded ominous."

Before we made it to our seats, the fire alarm sounded. In Nantucket, the fire alarm was a horn that let volunteer firemen know where to respond. When an alarm was pulled, the number of the box was transmitted and the horn sounded out the number. The volunteers kept a copy of the list in their trucks, which allowed them to go directly to the call instead of first going to the fire station.

The horn blared, paused, then blared again.

"Something strange is going on," I said as we hopped off the shuttle bus on Main Street.

Trucks of all kinds were racing up Main Street and turning onto Orange Street. Minutes later, another wave of emergency vehicles whizzed past us.

I heard someone yell, "There's been a plane crash at the airport!"

The next morning the town was abuzz about the Northeast Airlines plane that had crashed in the woods just beyond the runway. The word was that 83 people aboard, including all passengers and crew, were incinerated when the plane struck the trees and exploded. The pilots were attempting to land in the dense fog and couldn't find the runway. The aircraft had run out of options. The runways on the mainland and the island were socked in with fog. They had circled for a while hoping for a break in the weather but were running low on fuel. Pilots are trained that if they don't see the runway at 200 feet they are to abort. In this case, the pilots waited too long and caught the trees at the far end of the runway.

Out of curiosity, we took a drive out to the airport to see what we could see. We weren't the only lookie-loos. We ran into a traffic jam at the airport entrance.

From the access road we could see the burned-out section of forest and the mangled wreckage of Flight 93, pieces of the plane strewn about. I shuddered, thinking about the final moments for the passengers and crew. Lisa instinctively made the sign of the cross. We didn't get out of the truck. We'd seen enough. More than enough. To think about the lives lost and not only that—all the hearts connected to the deceased—all the lives disrupted, the ripple effect of such a tragedy. People who would never be the same, people whose hearts would always long for their loved one who fell out of the sky on a foggy night in Nantucket. I wondered if I knew anyone aboard that flight.

The next day, I learned that Seraphina Lima's fiancé and her father were on board. But it was a coincidence; they had yet to meet. Her fiancé had flown to Nantucket to meet the family for the first time and her father, Seraph, was returning from a business trip. Seraph had made the trip many times but always by boat. He had only flown because he was in a hurry to get back.

Seraphina's cousins, Cory and Genie Lima, had left the island for a better life. Her side of the family was not as light-complexed but she was fair-skinned and stunning, like a beauty queen or a model.

Seraphina's immediate family didn't get along with the Monteiros or Vieiras. They were prejudiced against their own people. Seraphina's father worked for a white family on the island, but no one was quite sure what he did. The Limas kept to themselves and didn't want their daughter playing with Kriolu kids. Her playmate was the daughter of a white family. The whole situation defied logic. Seraphina thought she was better than other Cape Verdeans, and she didn't care who knew it.

Seraphina had met her finance, Ralph, in Boston. The Piersons were a well-to-do colored family who lived in the wealthy part of Roxbury, close to Franklin Park. His father was a doctor and his son, Seraphina's soon-to-be husband, was a medical student. It was so up Seraphina's alley to become the wife of a doctor. But those dreams were lost to a foggy August night.

We got an earful when Aunt Mabel stopped by. I had secretly named Aunt Mabel *The Town Crier* which was also the name of the Nantucket newspaper. But Aunt Mabel often had the scoop before it made the paper.

"Seraph has always been stuck up and his wife Josephine is no better," Aunt Mabel began. Seraph was Aunt Mabel's age. They had even dated for a short time, but there was no love lost between them.

"Don't speak ill of the dead," said Mai, making the sign of the cross. "Their family must be devastated. I can't even imagine their loss."

"No good comes to people who disown their own race, their own family," said Aunt Mabel, ignoring Mai's advice. She had not come to gossip today as much as she had come to vent her feelings. She would not shed a tear for Seraph.

"What about Seraphina? Were they at the airport when the plane crashed?" asked Mai. "Kantu tristi!" how sad.

"She's her father's daughter. She's thinks she's too good to marry a Cape Verdean, especially one from Nantucket."

"All the young girls on the island feel that way," Mai, said, attempting to defend the bereaved.

"Well, I guess God had other plans for Seraphina."

Mai shook her head.

I had heard enough. People were just too hung up on color and race, light skin, and good looks. I was sick of hearing about it.

Lisa and I sat on our favorite spot on the beach at the end of Washington Street. After the conversation with Mai and Aunt Mabel, I was fired up about prejudice among our people. I'd been filling Lisa in on the pervasive nature of racism on Nantucket. "You know the Cape Verdeans are just as bad."

Lisa gave me a quizzical look.

"They're even worse, sometimes. They have more people to dislike, more targets."

I got the sense she really enjoyed our deeper conversations about matters of substance, consequence—that she was surprised by my worldly perspective. This egged me on and made me more animated.

"There's the brankus, the Merkanus di kor, and then there's the separate class of Portuguese who are brankus. Kriolus refer to them as Nhami-babu.

"Nhami-babu is a convoluted reference to people from the Azores, another set of Portuguese islands, where yams are one of the main agricultural products. It's a demeaning idiom suggesting that people from the Azores are all yam-pickers. At least that is how I interpreted its usage, though my command of Kriolu was imperfect because, at the time, the language was not codified in any document, making learning experiential. I spent my preschool years not knowing if a given spoken word was English or Kriolu.

"The crazy part of this anonymous bigotry is that Cape Verdeans and Azoreans often intermarry, and it is not only inter-island, it can be interracial as well. For example, my grandfather was from Fogo, one of the Cape Verde Islands, and my grandmother was from Santa Maria in the Azores. He was as dark as night and she was white as snow." I let that contradiction sink in. "So, if you get to know one, they're okay, but all the others are still yam-pickers." I paused to see if Lisa was grasping the nuance of Kriolu bigotry. "But it's even crazier than all that. Kriolus are even prejudiced against themselves.

"What's the difference between brankus' bigotry, and Kriolu racism? The ability to enforce your beliefs to the detriment of others. Kriolus were truly benign racists, the toothless tigers, while brankus had the ability to control the economy and thereby the lives of the people they were oppressing.

"I hear old folks talking about color all the time. The saying goes, 'if you're light, you're alright, if you're brown hang around, if you're black, get back.' And this comes from Cape Verdeans of all shades.

"It was too much for me. In fact, when I heard relatives talking like this, I would try to get them to see that they were doing, the very thing they accused brankus of doing—being prejudiced. But my pleas were largely ignored. They would say things like, 'He's just a kid. What does he know?' if they acknowledged me at all."

I realized I had been talking too much. "I'm sorry. I went on and on. It's just that I'm pretty passionate about exploring the hypocrisy."

"It's the same with my people. Probably all people, even whites."

I hopped up from our blanket and offered my hands to Lisa, gently pulling her up. Sitting in the sand without any support was killing my back. "Let's take a walk."

"Sure, but will you kiss me first?" she asked.

SIXTEEN

··

ANNA WALTZED INTO DANIEL'S ROOM LIKE SHE HAD something up her sleeve. He could tell almost immediately. He had been shuffling through boxes from his life and had discovered a poem he had long since forgotten. Strange how, after all the living one did, one's life was reduced to a stack of boxes. The problem with an archeological dig of one's life was that each letter, each keepsake, each document triggered a cascade of feelings.

"Sodade ta matam," he uttered to himself as she was walking in. He held a yellowed sheet of notebook paper that trembled in his grasp.

"N ka ta konprende." Anna said she didn't understand.

Daniel's face brightened. "Beautiful. Your accent is perfect!"

"Too bad my repertoire is so limited." She nabbed the chair from the corner and set it next to Daniel's.

"I'd be happy to teach you some more if you want. I mean, I'm not sure how useful it will be in your life, but at least you'll keep it alive when old fogies like me kick out."

"I'd love that! So, what does 'Sodade ta matam' mean?"

A sadness fell over Daniel's face and spread to his shoulders, which slumped.

"Oh, if you don't want to talk about it, we don't have to," she said, glancing away to give him privacy.

"It's just embarrassing. That's all."

"Well, I don't want to pry. Really."

"It means 'the longing is killing me.'"

"Is it related to the piece of paper you're holding?"

He nodded. "In part, yes. When you're my age, life turns into longing. Longing for the carefree days; longing for the people who have come and gone but who are still so alive in your heart; longing for the agile body and swift mind you once had. Also, there's another source. I think Cape Verdeans carry a longing for a land we never knew. We carry it deep in our hearts, and our minds seek to understand. It's like we lost something we never had. You know?"

"Actually, I do. I feel it, too. Sodade ta matam."

"It's music to my ears to hear you speak Kriolu so beautifully."

"Thank you. So, is that a poem, or something?"

"Hey! How did you know? You're a good sleuth."

"Nah, I'm not all that good. It's just that poetry often arises from yearning, from that place inside you that seeks to be filled."

Daniel smiled. It felt good to be seen. He had given up hoping that someone might see him again the way she did.

Anna shifted in her chair and looked like she wanted to say something. "Uh, I wanted to ask you something. But I want you to be completely honest with me. It won't hurt my feelings if you don't like my idea."

"Now, my curiosity is piqued!"

Anna glanced over at Lisa's photo. "Would you be willing to find her again?"

"Who?"

"Lisa?"

"Oh, no. That ship has sailed," he said, shaking his head vehemently.

"No worries. I just thought I'd ask. Because it's super easy these days to find people on the internet."

"I appreciate the thought, but no, thank you."

"Would you be willing to share your poem with me?"

"I've only shared it with one other person."

"With her?"

He nodded.

"If it's too personal, I understand."

He reconsidered. "You know what? I will share it, but it needs a little introduction."

Anna leaned in. "I'm all ears!"

I took Lisa to Surfside for a change of scenery and because it was the only beach with real waves. From town, it was a short distance to the south side of the island, which faced the Atlantic Ocean. A few cottages dotted the bluffs above the shifting dunes and swaying beach grass. Below the bluff was a steep drop-off to the beach. A hundred yards of beach stretched between the bluffs and the sea.

The beach was virtually empty, which was not uncommon. Unlike the in-town beaches, there was no lifeguard or facilities of any kind. So, if you got into trouble in the water, you were on your own.

We strolled down the path to the beach, my sights set on the waves. They were decent-sized waves and would be fun to play in.

I carried the cooler, Lisa toted the beach towels that would double as blankets.

"Boy, this place is beautiful," Lisa remarked after we had been sitting for a while. "What's out there: New Bedford?"

"No," I smiled. "New Bedford is on the other side. Straight across is maybe Portugal."

"You need to teach me how to speak Portuguese."

"You mean Kriolu."

"What's the difference?" she said, tying her hair back in a ponytail.

My ability to speak Kriolu was limited. There was typically no formal education offered to Kriolu children. One just picked it up by parroting the words and phrases spoken by family and community members.

"Portuguese is the language of commerce for the Cape Verde islands, while Kriolu is the language spoken at home and in the villages." I let that sink in before continuing. "Kriolu is spoken, not written. I have no idea how to spell anything besides 'jag.'" Jag was slang for jagacida, a dish made with rice and beans. "The good news is there are many everyday phrases that I can teach you." I listed many, including good morning, see you later, please, and thank you. "The language is crazy. For example, verbs don't get conjugated. The pronoun is used to determine the person and 'ka' is used to turn a statement negative."

"What about pronunciation? I hear you pronouncing 'j' real funny."

"In Spanish, you say, 'Jose' with an 'h' sound, for example. All your vowels are long. In Kriolu, they tend to be short and sometimes silent. So, for 'Jose,' the 'j' sound is like the last syllable of 'pleasure,' and the vowels are short like 'oh' and 'eh.' Try it."

Lisa gave it a try while I corrected her and tried to keep a straight face. When she almost had it, I said, "Try this one. 'Jaime.'"

She butchered it, and I chuckled again.

"Listen, if you're going to laugh at me, I'm not going to try," she pouted and crossed her arms.

"Oh, I'm sorry. I didn't mean to hurt your feelings."

Lisa cracked up. "I was kidding. Believe me, I'm not that sensitive. I mean, I'm Puerto Rican after all. Please continue, Dr. Monteiro."

I liked the sound of that. Dr. Monteiro. "Okay, remember the 'j' is like 'pleasure.' Spanish is staccato 'hi-me,' whereas Kriolu, like Portuguese, is more of a diphthong or a gliding vowel. The vowels run together. In fact, it's all one syllable."

Lisa frowned when I used the word "diphthong" and then she smiled.

I knew one of the things she loved about me was my command of English, which honestly, I didn't think was all that impressive. But perhaps I wasn't objective when it came to matters of myself.

"Try it again. It's the 'j' sound in 'pleasure' plus 'dime' without the 'd.' Jaime."

We were in hysterics as she trained her mind to say, "Jaime" in Kriolu instead of in Spanish. Her Spanish, like my Kriolu, was broken. But that didn't stop us from using our second languages.

When we were all laughed out about Jose and Jaime, I said, "Here's a good one. I have no clue how to spell this or what one of the uses actually means. 'Nha' is the word for 'my,' but it's also used to show respect to older women. For example, you remember the lady I introduced you to, who lives across from the beach, Nha Jule di Machine?"

189

"The woman with the black teeth and the pipe?" Lisa asked.

"That's the one." I smiled when Lisa described her.

Nha Jule was an ancient woman born in the old country whose husband had long since passed. She lived in a rickety shack with an outhouse in back. Her teeth were intact and straight but black as night from poor oral hygiene, Cape Verdean water, and her corn-cob pipe.

People young and old stopped by Nha Jule's house to visit and ask for her blessing. Cape Verdeans went out of their way to show respect for their elders. The conversations, although frequent, were neither long nor deep so as not to tax her. I had brought Lisa to meet Nha Jule on a trip to the beach at the end of Washington Street.

"In this case, 'Nha' doesn't mean 'my,' and it's not the word for Mrs., that's 'senhora,' but it's a sign of deference." Lisa smiled again, clearly impressed by my vocabulary.

"Oh, there's more. You don't just call her by her name. You assign her to her husband. Her husband's name was Machine, so you refer to her as Nha Jule di Machine. Get it?"

"Okay, professor, that's way more than I wanted to know, but very interesting. Want to go for a swim? Last one in is a rotten egg!"

No way was I going to be the rotten egg, so I jumped up and raced towards the waves. Lisa rushed to catch up as I dove in head-first, the cold water was a shock to my system. But my body quickly adapted. We played in the water like dolphins—diving, spinning, and doing summersaults. I could've stayed in the water with her forever, but a vigorous romp in the surf can be draining, so when we were thoroughly bushed, we plodded toward our spot on the beach and plunked down on our towels.

Lisa rested on her back, soaking in the warmth of the sand. "The sun feels good."

I reclined, too, mesmerized by the deep blue sky. My thoughts drifted to my Cape Verdean heritage and the old folks, like Nha Jule, who settled here. I could only imagine what her eyes had witnessed. Oh, the stories she could tell. But there was no asking her to remember the dark days. For her and others like her, Tiu Moxhe, Anna Jochim di Joao Tati, Joao Badiu, Nha Bebe, life on Nantucket was as good as they could hope for. As survivors of the diaspora their expectations were low. For them, the battle for survival was over, but in having escaped Cape Verde, the reality was anything but. The weary travelers had endured so much. On Nantucket, they were constrained by a lesser force but with an equally stifling impact.

My thoughts returned to Nha Jule. When I closed my eyes, I could see her. She wore on her wrinkled face heartache, pain, misery, and the loss that accompanies a lifetime of toil, trouble, and tragedy. It was there in plain sight in the etchings on her brow and cheeks, but yet she never spoke a word of it, nor did anyone who visited. She had survived. She had persevered. She had prevailed. She embodied the struggle that had heaved our people from Cape Verde and scattered us around the globe. She had no one, yet she had everyone.

Her extended and adopted family members stopped by to pay their respects, request her blessing, run her errands, or do her chores. She had earned the right through her endurance, tenacity, fortitude, and grace to be revered; to relax on her porch, smoke her pipe, and watch the passersby.

Cape Verdeans visited her each day, throughout the day, for short visits, but long enough to let her know she was loved. We paid our respects, but it was more than that. It was a thank you for enduring and making our lives possible. She was 100 years old, if she was a day. Although her face was wrinkled and her body shriveled, her eyes were as bright as a child's and her stain-toothed smile as warm as any open heart.

I hope we're up to the challenge to continue to prevail over adversity, I thought as I felt a moistness in the corner of my eyes.

There was so much folklore, tales spoken but not written, things that I had overheard and stories I'd been told about the old country, the struggles to survive, the separation of families as young men voyaged overseas to earn money to send back home. I heard stories of how Papai left Fogo at fifteen, never to see his family again, but sent money, food, and clothing home until he died. I never knew Peter Vieira, my maternal grandfather, but he came alive in my relatives' stories.

As I lay on the sand, the sun's rays warming my body, a vision came to me. This often happened when I allowed my mind to drift. Ideas arose in the form of evocative images. I saw my fifteen-year-old grandfather setting sail for America on the rough and rocky Atlantic to escape the starvation ravaging the islands.

I reached for Lisa's beach bag, where I had stashed my notepad and pen. I liked to keep them close in case something worth keeping popped into my mind. If I waited, the musings could be lost forever.

Lisa stirred when I reached over her. She lay on her stomach, tanning her back in a sun and sea reverie.

"Just grabbing something out of your beach bag."

She smiled and closed her eyes.

I sat up, balanced my notebook on my lap, and puzzled over a title for the poem coming to me in a burst of inspiration. I could see a shadowy peaked landscape in an azure sea off in the distance. It was the Cape Verde islands. *That's it! Nha Terra Longe, My Faraway Land.* Once I had the title, the words flowed faster than I could capture them, my scribbling barely legible.

Nha Terra Longe
(My Faraway Land)

We left in ships across the sea,
In search of life not liberty.
Some stayed behind who could not leave,
For those, our hearts still often grieve.
A family once in daily life,
Now torn apart by miles and strife.
We write and send what 'er we can,
From this new and distant land.
Our feelings mixed of our new home,
Though life is good, we feel alone.
Going back is a constant cry,
The yearning strong, I can't deny.
But life is here, a family new,
My wife, my sons, and daughters too.
The islands remain within my soul,
Perhaps I'll return before I go.
For now, I have the work at hand,
And will strive to prosper in this land.

Unlike so many poems that I had labored over and sometimes abandoned, this one poured out of me like a waterfall cascading over polished stones into a refreshing pool. It seemed divinely inspired, the words channeling through me; I was the vessel. Amazingly, the piece didn't require a second pass. As I rewrote it more legibly, I wondered if I could share it with Lisa. *Do I have the nerve? What if it's no good? What if she thinks my poetry stinks, but she feels pressured to compliment me?* I decided if she didn't like it, I'd say it was just my first pass and I planned to perfect it later. Despite doubts swirling, I nudged Lisa.

"Check this out. It just came to me while I was lying here." I had never shared my poetry with anyone, but Lisa was different. I shared so many things with her that I shared with no one else.

I couldn't help but gaze at her as she read my words. She seemed to be taking a long time, or was time passing slowly because I was anxious for her to like my work?

She glanced up from the page filled with my words, etchings of my soul. "Oh, Danny, that's so beautiful."

Do I see admiration in her eyes or am I just imagining things?

"I love the rhythm, the bittersweet melancholy, the feeling that you're in two places at once and not fully satisfied with either. The yearning is palpable."

"You think?" I said, lacking confidence in my writing ability, feeling vulnerable and exposed.

She cradled my cheek with her hand. "You have a gift," she assured me, "a real talent!"

And for a moment, I believed her.

SEVENTEEN

....

W E WERE RELAXING AT THE BEACH AT THE END OF Washington Street. We hadn't been here in a while. We sat by ourselves next to the fence that demarked the private property.

I was telling Lisa about Aunt Mabel's diatribe launched against Seraph and his family. "She was driving nails in his coffin."

"What does she have against him?"

"I don't know specifically. There's a lot of history there. It was all before my time but, the straw that broke the camel's back, and I only heard this through the grapevine, was that Seraph called Aunt Mabel's youngest son, Anthony, a homosexual and word got back to Aunt Mabel."

"Well, is he?" Lisa asked.

"Very. He's a flamboyant dresser, effeminate in his mannerisms, and vocal about his preferences, but it's not something you say to Aunt Mabel if you value your life. Apparently, Anthony was caught with another guy in the boatyard and Seraph couldn't stop gossiping about it."

"Where is he now?"

"Aunt Mabel shipped him off to New Bedford. It's a topic everyone avoids."

I needed to stretch my legs after sitting in the sand, which I often found to be exceedingly uncomfortable. I pulled Lisa up, and we sauntered to the water's edge. I dug around in the sand, looking for flat rocks to skim. "A-ha!" I said when I found a perfect skipping stone. I whipped it side-arm across the water. It skipped, one, two, three, four times before it lost momentum and sank to the bottom. "Bet you can't beat that!"

Lisa found a rock and tried her hand skipping but her stone sunk like a lead weight.

"No, no, no! Okay, first, you have to find a good skipping stone—flat and smooth." He handed her one he had found. "Then, you must use the side-arm technique, like so." He demonstrated and each time his rock skipped, he counted aloud."

"Oh, showoff!" she said. Lisa tried again and again. Finally, she managed to hurl a stone that skipped three times. She threw her hands up in victory and around my shoulders. "See? I'm not a rock-skipping loser! I mean, you've had your entire life to perfect this very important life skill."

I kissed her cheek, laughing. "You're a quick study!" Suddenly out of the corner of my eye, I spotted some familiar boats out in the harbor. "Look! It's the Rainbow fleet."

"What's that?" Lisa asked.

The Rainbow was a twelve-foot four-inch gaff-rigged catboat.

"From what I've read, the Nantucket Yacht Club brought them here in 1926 to set up a racing fleet for young kids. Each has a sail of different color so the parents can track their kid out on the water."

"You weren't one of those kids. Were you?" Lisa asked, already knowing the answer.

"Are you kidding me? Have you noticed the color of my skin? They're nice to watch, though."

"This must have been a tough place growing up, seeing all the trappings of wealth beyond your reach." Lisa was clearly saddened by the thought. "Enough of this depressing talk," she said, turning her back to the Rainbow fleet and walking toward her towel, lying on the sand. I was a few steps behind, but I caught up to her.

"What were you and Marie talking about the other day?"

"She was asking me about my family and my job and about us," Lisa said.

"What did you tell her about us?"

"Your whole family wants to know what will become of us come Labor Day."

"They were hoping that you would just fade away, but I think they've given up on that notion," I said.

"What are we going to do?" she asked, giving me a serious look.

"You're going to go back to work at the law firm and I'll be a starving writer."

"Seriously, Danny."

"I'm serious. If you want me to come with you, that is."

Lisa jumped on me, pushing me over onto the sand. "You'd better not be toying with my heart."

"I'm not," I said, pretending to struggle to break free from her wrist-hold. "I would never do that!"

She climbed on top of me while she held me down and we kissed. She looked up to see that others were watching, so she rolled off me and sat on her towel. "Darn voyeurs!"

When I sat up, she helped me brush the sand out of my hair.

"I'm going to tell Terry she needs to find another roommate," Lisa said.

"That'll go over well."

"I really don't care at this point. She hasn't been a good friend through this whole situation. Whatever she has against you is her problem, not mine."

"Do your parents know about me?"

"Well, yes and no."

"That clears that up," I said in jest.

"I'm real close with my mom. I told her all about you while I was home. She was glad to hear that I wasn't seeing Tony anymore."

"Your mother knew about Tony?!" I said, incredulously.

"I told you. We are very close."

"And your dad?"

"If he knew about Tony, he'd kill him," said Lisa.

"And me."

"You'll meet him."

I was filled with dread at the thought.

"He'll like you. You're both know-it-alls," she said, laughing. "So, when are you going to tell your parents about our plans?"

Her question hit me like a punch in the gut, taking my breath away. It wasn't that I wasn't planning to go to New York. It was just that bringing my parents into the equation made it undeniably real and that much scarier. "Uh, I guess I hadn't thought about it." I shrugged.

She stopped and confronted me with her eyes. "Are you planning to back out?"

"No, why?"

"Well, it's like you're not taking it seriously, taking us seriously," she said, her hands on her hips.

I sighed. "It's not that. It's…"

"It's what?" she looked panic-stricken, searching for my eyes, which gazed past her.

"I don't know how to tell them without disappointing them."

"Danny, part of growing up *is* disappointing your parents. It goes with the territory. That's how you know you're an adult."

I didn't like that she was lecturing me about becoming an adult like I was just a naïve kid with no life experience. "I know," I said, in my best condescending tone.

She held me steady with a hand placed on each arm and asked, "Do you?"

It was hard to get Mai and Pai together at the same time. Pai was gone most of the day, working at one job or another. And I worked the dinner shift. By the time I got off, Pai was already tucked in for the night. I needed to find the right time. I couldn't do it in the morning when Pai was focused on getting out the door to his first job of the day. It was going to have to be after dinner.

I hoped I could put it off forever and then kind of disappear. But I knew that was the cowardly option. Plus, Mai would never forgive me.

I told my boss that I was going to need to get off an hour early, which went over like a lead balloon.

"That's our busiest time," she said.

"I've asked the girls to cover for me." The waitresses liked me and were more than willing to cover for me. "I'll come in early tomorrow and set everything up before we open for breakfast. This is an important family matter," I said.

When the clock struck 8:00 pm, I bolted out the door. I got home slightly winded from my dash down Washington Street. I hardly noticed the dense fog. My mind was running over the conversation with Mai and Pai as quickly as my feet hit the pavement. As I approached the front door, I paused to catch my breath.

Pai was sitting in his easy chair, reading the paper. Mai sat across from him with rosary beads in hand.

"Danny, you're home early," said Mai.

"I need to talk to you and I wanted to catch Pai before he went to bed."

"What's this about?" she asked, slightly alarmed.

"It's about him and that girl," said Pai, not looking up from his paper.

"Lisa, her name is Lisa," I said, annoyed that Pai refused to remember her name.

Pai folded the paper and set it on the table. "I'm all ears. What's so important that you had to leave work early? It doesn't look good when an employee does that, you know."

Pai's work ethic made him every employer's dream. He believed your job came first, always do your best, leave no room for your boss to complain about your work, be on time, and earn a fair wage for an honest day's work. Pai was a work machine. He had no social life and very little family life. He was, first and foremost, a provider. It was rare if Pai wasn't working two or more jobs—scalloping, short-order cook, gardener, carpenter, chief cook, and bottle washer. He did it all and never once complained.

I glanced at Mai and then across the room at Pai. I inhaled deeply, my heart racing. *Say it. Just say it!* "After Labor Day, I'm going to New York with Lisa." I waited and watched my parents, who appeared to be frozen. Flight, fight, freeze—the body's physiological reaction to a perceived harmful event, attack, or threat to survival. *Was this a threat to their survival? Did they perceive harm to them or me?*

Mai was the first to speak. She flung her hands down to her lap. "Do you even know what you're doing? Have you thought this through? You've never been any further than New Bedford."

"I have to grow up sometime. I can't stay here. I can't do the kind of work that Pai does. I'm not cut out for it." My gaze dropped and my head hung low. I was embarrassed to admit what I had always known to be true. I was not the man my father was and would never be.

"Your father and I already know that. We know you're different than your brothers but New York? Are you sure you're ready to take such a big step?"

I blurted out without thinking, "I love Lisa and we want to be together."

"I knew that this was about a girl," said Pai, who had been silent until I mentioned Lisa. "How well do you know this girl?"

"Lisa. Her name is Lisa," I interjected, wanting Pai to acknowledge her name.

But Pai purposefully avoided saying her name. He wanted it to remain impersonal, distant even. "What do you know about her,

her family, her background? What if it turns out she has some condition, some illness that will require you to take care of her for the rest of your life? Are you prepared for that?"

I had no idea where Pai was going with this thread. *Who knows what the future holds for anyone? If you love someone, you take your chances, for better or for worse—right?*

"You mean to tell me that you wouldn't have married Mai, if you found out she might get sick because she had some inherited trait?" I started to say, "congenital disease," but I was sure Pai's English wasn't that good.

Mai, looked at Pai, waiting for his answer, but none was forthcoming.

"N ta da bo un Konsedju," I'm going to give you some advice. He continued speaking in Kriolu. "The choices we make early in our lives will follow us throughout the years. The sweet can sour with the passage of time; joy can turn to sorrow. Regret is a bitter pill to swallow." He paused for a long moment. I knew what was coming next. I had heard it a million times, *e bo ki sabe,* it's you who knows—best—is implied, but in reality it's a sarcastic comment meaning just the opposite, *you think you're so smart.*

There was a superstition (one of many) among the folks from the old country, those who were part of the diaspora, who had seen the poverty, the starvation, the deaths by the thousands in Cape Verde. They subconsciously and overtly believed that they were not entitled to too much happiness, evidenced by their history. Whenever they saw anyone appearing to be overly happy, they would caution, "Dia di sabi e ves di fedi," an idiom, loosely translated, too much joy leads to sorrow. Or, simply put, laugh today, cry tomorrow.

My father was a man of few words, and when he spoke, he often spoke in riddles. For example, if he wanted to tell you that you weren't listening to him, he would say, "N ta papia pedra bo ta kudi pou," I'm talking about stones and you're answering about sticks.

I tried to decipher Pai's cryptic message to figure out how to respond. Finally, I said, "I've got to make my own mistakes. Like Mai says all the time, 'you make your bed; you have to lie in it.' Nobody can make my choices for me."

With those words, Mai teared up and pulled out the hanky she always kept up her sleeve. She mopped her eyes as if catching her tears before they escaped down her cheeks.

It broke my heart to cause her sorrow. I wanted to say something that might comfort her, like, *okay, I won't go. I'll just stay here forever.* But, as Lisa had said, this was part of growing up—making your mother cry. It didn't seem fair.

That was Pai's cue. "Time for bed. Have to be up early." And he shuffled off, shaking his head at me.

Mai and I continued talking. Through her sniffles, she managed to say she was happy for me but sorry that I'd be leaving the family. "It just won't be the same without you here," she said.

I assured her that Lisa and I would come to visit.

Mai got up and waved for me to come toward her. She embraced me like she'd never let go, like it was the last time she'd ever see me, like she was preparing to say goodbye to her baby boy.

EIGHTEEN

···

SHE BEGAN TAPPING GENTLY AT MY WINDOW AROUND
2:30 am. Her constant rapping was at first too subtle to awaken me,
but she persisted. I dreamed I was on a ship at sea, the tapping
sound of the halyard repeatedly striking the towering mast. The
ship lurched against six-foot waves and settled in the troughs. At
the captain's command, I was pursuing a whale, even though I had
no intention of harming him.

By 3:00 am, the gentle tapping gave way to a more insistent rat-
tling and then a pounding on the window and the walls on the
south side of the house. She was determined to be heard, to be
acknowledged. After all, she had traveled a long way. Her journey
began many days ago near the Cape Verde Islands, taking a cir-
cuitous route west and then north, following a course traveled by
many of her antecedents who had departed those islands in years
past. She and I were not acquainted, but we would come to know
each other well before the day was done. Would she be a tempestuous sort, leaving behind a destructive wake?

The area around the Cape Verde Islands is a cauldron for
cooking up Atlantic storms; the hot, dry air off the Sahara Desert
mixes with the cool, moist air of the Atlantic and combines with
the African easterly jet stream to make the perfect stew. Not all

hurricanes that form in the Atlantic originate near Cape Verde. It is true for most major hurricanes that have impacted the continental United States. This unnamed new arrival to the shores of Nantucket was one of them. She was anonymous because the naming convention did not start until 1953.

I was awakened by a strong wind gust that overturned an empty wheelbarrow in the yard under my window. The gust sent it screeching across the walkway and banging against the stairs leading to the back kitchen.

It took me a few seconds to shake off my drowsiness and to realize what was happening. I had heard murmurings of an approaching hurricane and had seen the red triangular gale warning flags flying off the coastguard station at Brant Point but had thought nothing more of it. Storms came and went this time of year, usually resulting in the loss of a beach day and nothing more. But you never knew until they made landfall.

I sat up on the edge of my bed, checking the clock on the nightstand. It was 5:15 am. I could feel the wind picking up. The house was old and the window in my bedroom danced as the driving rain pounded against it in waves. Sheets of water cascaded down. I knew I couldn't go back to sleep, so I dressed and plodded down to the kitchen. When I opened the hallway door, I could see lights on in the kitchen. Pai was dressed in his oilskins and about to head out the door.

Oilskin is a heavy cloth material which has been made waterproof by being impregnated with a mixture of hot wax, oil and gum, and is the traditional foul weather gear worn by fishermen and sailors.

"Danny, get dressed." This meant suiting up in my foul weather gear, hooded jacket, bib, and boots. "I'm going to need you to help me down at the wharf. We have to check on Michael's boat. This storm looks like a bad one."

"Have you checked the weather report?" I asked.

"They said 75 mph winds with gusts up to 90."

We arrived at the commercial wharf with hardly a glimmer of daylight. When Pai opened his truck door, the wind nearly ripped the door off its hinges. It prevented me, on the passenger's side, from opening my door at all. I climbed over the seat to Pai's door to get out. We gingerly navigated our way to the boardwalk using the scallop shanties as a windbreak. Once on the wharf, we navigated from piling to piling, lashed by the wind, to the finger dock that led to where Michael's boat, *Cretcheu*, was tied up. The water in the slip area was calm compared to the harbor, but the waves still tossed the boat around. *Cretcheu* was tied up in the middle of the docking area, so it was fairing okay. One boat tied up at the entrance had sunk and was held up only by a bowline. With only the white bow protruding from the water, it looked like an iceberg in the dim morning light.

"Danny, grab the spring line and take up the slack," Pai yelled over the howling wind. "I'm going to start the bilge pump. Get a couple more fenders. See if you can keep the boat from pounding against the dock."

I was working as quickly as I could, my eyes squinted and head bowed against the lashing rain.

After about thirty minutes of lashing down the lines, pumping water out of the bilge, adjusting all the fenders, and securing the cabin, there was nothing left to do so, we braced ourselves against the wind and headed back to the truck. The dock and the pilings were slippery, and my hands wet and cold. As I reached for a piling, my reach wasn't synchronized with my grip, and my partially-opened hand crashed against the piling, causing a sharp pain to radiate up my arm. It sent me into a side spin just as a gust whipped me around and threw me off-balance. As I attempted to plant my feet, I realized I was in the space between the dock and a large catboat. The tide was up, so the boat was almost even with the dock. I tried to step on the gunwale as I pivoted to grab the piling, but I missed the handhold and slid into the cold, dark water between the dock and the boat. Pai, who was leading the way, was unaware of my mishap until he heard me cry out.

"Pai! Help, Pai!" The weight of my foul weather gear and boots quickly filling with water weighed me down as I struggled to stay at the surface.

When Pai turned around, he couldn't see me and had no idea how far behind him I was. He was cautiously backtracking when I, like a great white whale, broke the water's surface. "Pai, help! Help!"

Before Pai could reach me, I went under for a second time, pulled down by the weight of my gear. I realized the gear, designed to protect me on land, was a liability in the water. With it on, I could become another casualty of the sea. I quickly slipped off my boots and flutter-kicked to the surface, where I gasped for air. Pai knew I was a good swimmer and was ready when I surfaced the second time. We locked arms, and Pai raised me high enough to reach the gunwale on the catboat to pull myself out of the water.

The adrenaline coursing through my body provided a much-needed boost to save me from the hungry jaws of the sea—the jaws that had swallowed many a sailor and swimmer, the jaws of the deep that weren't going to consume me. Not that day.

When Pai and I returned home, Mai, Marie, Eugenia, and Michael Jr. were sitting around the kitchen table, eating breakfast. I was soaked and a bit shaken.

"What happened to you? You look like a drowned rat!" said Marie.

"He went overboard," said Pai, nonchalantly, pulling off his boots.

"Oh, for heaven's sake! You know better than to go out in this weather!" Mai said with a scowl. "You weren't born and raised on an island for nothing."

It was scary for a moment, but I was never in any real danger of drowning. Thankfully, I had the presence of mind to yank off the boots and swim toward the surface. Of course, I wouldn't share any of these details with Mai. Although, I planned to dramatize the story for Lisa to see her reaction.

"Had to take care of Michael's boat," offered Pai.

"That darned boat is cursed! The sooner we get rid of it, the better." Mai shot Pai a disapproving glance and said nothing more on the subject. Sometimes silence drove home one's point better than words. She turned to me and said, "Get out of those wet clothes! You'll catch a death-a-cold."

It wasn't until she said those words that I noticed I was shivering. I ran up to my room. I quickly changed and headed back to the kitchen. I wolfed down a bowl of Cheeri Oats and left for work. On bad weather days, the restaurant was always crowded, and people tended to linger, so I didn't get off work until after 1:00 pm.

By now, the storm was getting serious; the wind thrashing the trees, limbs cracking off and littering the roads—casualties of Mother Nature's wrath. Main Street was deserted; just a few hardy types were out and about. Weather forecasting was virtually non-existent back then, but weather reports of actual conditions were broadcast on the radio. They reported winds close to 90 mph with gusts over 100!

The wind nudged me along as I hurried down Main Street. It appeared that the island was between rain bands, at least in my location. Since it was on the way, I decided to check on *Cretcheu* to see if the bilge needed pumping again. I also wanted to see the whitecaps in the harbor in the daylight. Unlike most people, I loved walking the beach during hurricanes; it was invigorating to commune with nature when it was tempestuous. To witness the power and might of the natural world was humbling and awe-inspiring. It brought me comfort somehow.

I strolled past the ice plant. Crazy Ernie wasn't outside. *He wasn't that crazy.* I could feel the wind at my back, nudging me along, forcing my steps. On the opposite side of the scallop shanties were wharf cottages. Jutting out from the corner building, I spotted a sailboat mast dangling at a 45-degree angle, so I crossed the street to see what was going on. As the pier on that side of the wharf came into view, a could see the 40-foot sailboat listing on its side, the hull smashed up. It appeared only to be afloat because of the lines tied to the dock. Beside the vessel was a man attempting to photograph the dying beast as waves splashed up against the dock and sprayed over him. He continued undeterred. I figured, *got to get those insurance photos at all costs.* I crossed back to the scallop-shanty side of the wharf.

Seeing that the *Cretcheu* was riding out the storm, I started for home. When I arrived, Lisa was there waiting for me.

"Alice dropped me off on her way to work. I heard you went swimming this morning without me," she joked.

"Yeah, I could have easily drowned," I dramatized. "In fact, maybe I did, and you're talking to my ghost." I made a ghoulish face and wailed hauntingly. "Oooohh!"

She laughed. "Oh, you don't scare me, even if you are a ghost! Tell me what happened."

I drew upon my literary skills to conjure up a harrowing tale of my near-death experience. "It was the man versus the sea, the tale that has been told throughout time, as long as man has graced the planet. But, unlike so many others, I took on the sea and won," I concluded with dramatic flair.

We shared a hearty laugh. She knew I was making the story more colorful for her sake.

"I'm so glad you survived to tell the tale!" she said.

"Hey, I have an idea!"

"Uh-oh. Danny has an idea. This can't be good," she said, laughing.

"Let's go take a walk on the beach."

"You've got to be kidding," Lisa said with a smirk.

"No, I'm serious. It's exhilarating to feel the power of nature when you're not in any danger."

"Until you are and you get swept out to sea, never to be seen again. I can just see the headline, 'Young Lovebirds Carried by Storm to Their Untimely Deaths.'"

I laughed. "Nothing like that will happen. If anything, we'll be pushed around by some gusts and get sprinkled on. But a little wind and rain never hurt anyone."

Youth knew no real caution, so it didn't take much for me to convince her to venture out into the wild weather.

As we headed down to the beach at the end of Washington Street, I decided to stopped in and check on Nha Jule di Machine. She was curled up on her sofa covered by a hand-knit blanket, drinking tea from a pink and white china pot, pipe in her mouth, reading. Her place smelled of black tea, earthy, floral and sweet. The book she held trembled in her hands. Upon closer inspection, I saw she was reading *Moby Dick*.

"Has Captain Ahab died yet?" I asked.

"Oh, Danny, don't ruin it for me!" she smiled.

But I knew she had read it many times. "Oh, sorry. Silly me!"

When Nha Jule arrived from the old country she was unable to speak or read English. Like most Cape Verdeans, she was self-taught. In later years TV soap operas were the vehicle for learning English but for Nha Jule's generation there were only books. Moby Dick was her primer.

She leaned in. "I'm rooting for Moby Dick! Can't men just leave whales be? They have to meddle. Don't they? I don't blame Moby one bit for taking Ahab's leg. Heck, he should've just polished him off!"

Lisa and I chuckled.

"Did you do okay in the storm?" I asked.

"Oh, it was nothing." She swatted the air, pipe in hand. "Now, the Yankee Clipper... That was a real blower! Remember that one?"

"How could I forget?"

Nha Jule's face froze in guilt. "Desculpam!" Forgive me. She pointed toward the teapot on the table, her hand trembling slightly. "Mininus, toma un xikra di xa," Children, have a cup of tea.

"No thank you. We just wanted to stop by to make sure you were okay," I said.

"Alright, then. I'll just get back to my reading. Oh, Danny, who's your favorite character?"

I knew this was a test. "Gabriel, the prophet." Gabriel, the prophet, had predicted doom for anyone who threatened Moby Dick. His predictions seemed to carry some weight, as those aboard his ship who had hunted the whale had met disaster.

She was pleased. "Mine, too. Well, other than the whale."

Lisa and I were casually walking hand-in-hand as close to the water's edge as possible. "What did Nha Jule say to you in Kriolu?" Lisa asked, proud of her pronunciation.

"She offered us a cup of tea. She also called us children." I smiled. "It's just something old folks do. It's more a term of endearment than about age."

"Being that old has to be hard," Lisa said pensively.

It was low tide, so the waves were breaking a long way from shore and gently rolling up onto the beach. The winds had significantly subsided.

"The worst hurricane we've had here hit well after Labor Day, in 1938. It was nicknamed, 'The Yankee Clipper.' It was a Category 3 with winds over 110 mph."

"Wow! That's nuts!"

We were on the beach close to my house. I pointed to it across the street. "The area from here, past our house, and up Lafayette Street was under several feet of water. We had to stay on Upper Orange Street for a couple of days with Aunt Alice until the water receded. At 110 mph, the winds would knock you off your feet. That one was a scary storm. This is just a little rainstorm in comparison." I smirked.

"What's going on with those boats on the beach?" Lisa referred to a couple of small vessels that had washed ashore.

"When the wind kicks up, moorings break loose, and the waves beach the boats. They should be okay once the storm's over. Hey, look at that," I said, pointing toward the sky where silvery light filtered through the angry clouds. "The storm is breaking. There's going to be a great sunset. You know what they say, 'Red sky at night, a sailor's delight.'"

"Is that true or just Cape Verdean superstition?" Lisa asked half-jokingly.

"Within limits, I'd say, there's truth in those words, but I'm just a country boy from Nantucket. What do I know?"

"You know plenty. That's one of the things I love about you, Danny Monteiro."

We turned to gaze deeply into each other's eyes, embracing and sharing a lingering kiss as a passing shower anointed our union. The moment felt sacred, and like it might never come again.

NINETEEN

·······························

"How are you, handsome?" Anna had taken to kissing Daniel's cheek in greeting. The small act of affection made his day, although he would never admit this to her. Not in a million years. He refused to succumb to the cliché of a lonely old man, even though that was how he felt at times.

She brought in the damp cold and the scent of the falling leaves. It wasn't an unpleasant smell, just one of earthy decay—things returning to the earth from whence they came. He remembered strolling the island streets when there was a chill in the air, brilliantly colored leaves overhead and underfoot, and the smell of apple pies baking in every home. Fall was apple pie season, and whenever he stopped in for a visit at anyone's home, he was always offered fresh, warm apple pie a la mode. How the sweet, tangy apples and the buttery crust with vanilla ice cream tickled his tastebuds. He could practically taste it.

"I brought you a surprise," she said, holding something behind her back. "Which hand?"

"Let's see. I'll go with the left."

"Nope."

"Doggone. So, I don't get the surprise because I guessed wrong?"

"You get one more guess." She grinned.

"Ha! That's too easy. The right!"

She whipped out a tinfoil-covered pie tin.

"Oh, my word. Is that what I think it is?"

"Apple pie made from freshly picked apples," she said as she ripped off the tinfoil.

His eyes widened with delight. "Well, now, that's uncanny. You read my mind!"

"I remember your saying you loved apple pie."

"Oh, dear. I don't remember that at all."

"That's okay. I'll pick up the slack for rememberin' things. You have so much life to keep track of; I can see why things fall through the cracks."

"Now is that a polite way of saying I'm an old geezer?"

She laughed.

Daniel glanced down. "Shall we try some pie?"

After Anna had scored some ice cream and had heated the pie in Our Island Home's microwave, she served it to Daniel.

He took a big whiff and closed his eyes. Then he plunged his fork into the pie and relished his first bite. "Well, this is the best thing I've ever eaten in all my life!"

"I'm not sure it deserves that level of praise but thank you—my mama's recipe. The secret is butter. Lots of butter."

"I used to pick apples. I used to do a lot of things before this," Daniel said, motioning toward his legs. "Then everything changed."

Anna peered at Daniel then down at her pie. Her face softened, her eyes seeking. She asked in a near-whisper as if inching toward a secret, "What happened?"

Nantucket wasn't very big. There were only so many places one could go, and then one ran out of real estate. I wanted to make sure to show Lisa the entire island. Who knew when we would be back after this summer?

"Do you like to fish?" I asked, one day.

She laughed. "That's a funny question. I've never been fishing, so I can't say."

"Well, we're going blue fishing, then."

I had learned three ways to fish for blues. You could troll for blues from a boat. You could fish for blues off the pier, or my favorite way to catch them—surfcasting. There was an art to surfcasting for bluefish. First, you had to catch them when they were running. They were always moving, either due to the water temperature or the location of the baitfish. There were two things to look for—the boiling water caused by a bluefish feeding frenzy or circling gulls diving on the baitfish. Then you needed the right lure and the ability to cast right into the middle of the action. Surfcasting was the closest poor people came to the thrill of deep-sea fishing.

I loaded the fishing gear in the truck, and we headed up Main Street to Madaket Path Road and followed it for six miles until we reached the Atlantic Ocean. Madaket was on the far west coast, and the place we were headed was a stretch of beach at the end of Madaket Harbor.

We had to park and walk a ways to reach the perfect spot. I set down my gear and checked the water and sky. No birds and no boiling.

"Guess we're going to have to wait a while until the tide chang-es. Once the tide starts to come in, it will draw the baitfish, and the blues will follow."

Lisa smiled as if to say, *okay, whatever you say*. Lisa spread out the blanket and took a seat, hands on her knees, looking around at the beach, on a lovely day with virtually no one else in sight. "Don't people come to this beach?" she asked.

"It's too far out of town for the day-trippers. The locals will be here in the evening. Fishing is even better then."

After sitting and waiting for a while, I decided to try my luck at fishing even though there was neither boiling water nor circling gulls.

We walked down to the shoreline. I carried my pole and bait box full of lures.

Trying to impress Lisa, I said, "The secret to catching blues is the right lure." I opened the box to reveal a collection of them.

"I like to use this shiner." I pulled it out and attached it to my line. "Let me show you how it's done. First you need to open the reel latch, here, to allow it to free wheel, put your thumb over here to hold it, until you cast and then you take the rod back and snap it like a whip, pointing the tip toward your target. Once the lure hits the water you flip the latch back like that. Simple huh?" I cast the lure a good distance into the murky water. I convinced Lisa to give it a try. But she was hopeless and soon gave up.

"I'm better at eating fish," she laughed. "If you catch something, are you going to fry it up for me?"

I nodded, half-listening, because my attention was fixed on the gulls that had gathered and were diving in a fixed location in the water. "Look, over there," I said, pointing further down the beach. I quickly reeled in my line and ran down the shoreline. When I arrived directly opposite of where the birds were diving, I could see the disturbance in the water.

"They're here!" I cast my lure directly into the center of the action. Bingo! I started reeling in the line like I was possessed and immediately sent it back out. I did this at least a half-dozen times. On the next cast, the lure hit the water, and the pole bent to indicate something was pulling on it.

"I got one!" I yelled and released the catch on the rod to give the fish some line before I set the hook. What happened next wasn't clear, but the fish was running for deep water with my line and lure. I flipped the catch to stop the line and began reeling it in. My arm whirled around the rod, cranking for all I was worth. I watched the water for a sign that the fish was coming closer, but it didn't seem to be. On impulse, I decided to land the fish by running up the beach. Keeping the line taut, I took off at a full gallop across the flat sand until the fish flapped on the shore.

Lisa's pearls of laughter rose above the rhythm of the sea. She didn't know much about fishing, but she could see this wasn't the conventional way to catch a bluefish or any fish for that matter. She was in hysterics watching me running up the beach, fishing pole in hand, like a lunatic.

"I wasn't letting this one get away," I said, slightly embarrassed by my unorthodox, no-holds-barred fishing technique.

When the fish was safely secured in the pail and flapping around for dear life, we both had a good laugh, recounting the episode.

"Wait until I tell your father!"

"Don't you dare! I'll never live it down."

It was getting late and I had to be to work by 5:00 pm, so we packed up and headed back to town.

I had plans for that bluefish but it was going to have to wait until tomorrow. Bluefish is an acquired taste, as you know. I was taught to broil it with a heavy coating of mayonnaise to absorb the oiliness of the fish and bring out the flavor. It worked every time.

Just past the turn by the cleaners, I could see all the way down Washington Street to my house. For some strange reason, there were a bunch of cars parked on our side of the street. Nobody ever parked there because it blocked traffic. People, like Aunt Mabel, even parked on the other side as far off the road as possible.

"Something's up," I said to Lisa, who had no idea what I was talking about. "What are all these cars doing here?"

There was no place for me to park, so I turned on to Lafayette Street only to discover that cars were parked on that street as well. *What the heck is going on?* I pulled the truck into the field up the street, left everything in it, grabbed Lisa by the hand, and dashed for the back door.

When we walked in, Marie, Joseph, Sarah, Aunt Mabel, Alice, and several other people were standing around. *Is this an impromptu party, or did something happen?* I knew the answer but I didn't want to accept it. "Where's Mai?" I asked, panicked.

"She's lying down," said Marie.

Seeing everyone but Pai, I asked, "Where's Pai?" I expected someone to say he was working. The silence went on a little too long, so I knew he wasn't working.

"Danny," Marie said, "Pai had a stroke."

"What? Where is he? At the hospital?"

"Pai's dead, Danny. He collapsed on Main Street. They tried to revive him, but he was already gone."

A wave of incredulity washed over me. Pai couldn't be dead. He was invincible. I hadn't realized until now that I had expected him to live forever. "Are you sure?"

She nodded, her arms tightly crossed over her chest as if trying to hold herself together.

My first feeling was numbness, then nausea and disorientation. *I didn't get to say goodbye.* I looked at my sister and steeled myself before asking, "How's Mai doing?"

Marie started to speak but then was overcome by grief. She hid her face in her hands and sobbed.

I went to her and placed my hand on her shoulder to let her know she wasn't alone—that I was right there with her.

Lisa quietly approached and embraced me from behind, not saying a word; she just held me close, her arms around my waist. I knew she could feel my chest heaving as I braced against my deep sorrow.

People slowly migrated from the kitchen to the living room, leaving Lisa and me alone. I was seated, and Lisa stood behind me with her hand on my shoulder, allowing me to grieve.

I reached up and placed my hand over hers to let her know I appreciated her being there. We didn't speak for the longest time. The feelings communicated through our hands said all we needed to say. *I love you. I'm here for you. You can count on me.*

I don't recall how I made it through the rest of the day. It was a blur of burning eyes, shallow breath, and a queasy stomach. I felt suddenly rudderless and couldn't find my bearings. I hadn't realized how much I depended on Pai to feel that all was right with the world.

I had missed another day of work, and my boss was not pleased. When I explained to her that my father had died, she was surprisingly less than compassionate. *Where was the woman who had hired me?* She seemed indifferent. But on the other hand, I got it. She had a business to run. Summer was only 13 weeks, and she needed to make her money while she could. *But my father died, for God's sake. Are others' lives that insignificant?* I never returned to the Pleasant Inn after that day.

I wanted to know what had happened to Pai. I had to see the place where he had died. I needed to understand why no one had stopped to help him until Uncle Roy happened by and saw him crumpled on the sidewalk. *How long had he been there? Would he be alive if someone had rendered first aid?* Sadly, these questions would never be answered.

The next day, Lisa and I walked to the spot where Pai was found. It wasn't on Main Street but rather on the corner of Washington and Main. At that location, there is a compass rose on the side of a building depicting Nantucket's place in the world. It was crafted on the side of H. Marshall Gardiner's store in the early 1930s to bring business to his store and others. Visitors to Nantucket often stopped at the corner of Washington and Main to get their bearings while trying to figure out how to get to Siasconset or Surfside. As well as Moscow, Paris, and Calcutta. It was the perfect place for a commemorative photo, and many day-trippers struck poses for the camera.

Why wasn't anyone there to help Pai? And if people had been there, why didn't they help him? Because he was colored? Because his life was less worthy? I was angry, but I didn't know at whom to be angry. I needed someone to blame for this. Was it Pai's fault for working himself to death? Was it the circumstances that dictated he did so to provide for his family? Or was it indicative of life to end unceremoniously? Just like that—after all the trying, striving, hustling, hurrying, working, living, loving, life was extinguished, out like a candle. And life went on without that person. Only a small circle of folks felt the absence. But they eventually moved on, too. And the hole left by the deceased got smaller and smaller until it vanished.

Lisa was concerned that Pai's death would affect my decision to leave with her come Labor Day, but she didn't make a big deal of her concerns. "I hope you're still coming, but I totally understand if you want to postpone."

I was now more determined than ever to put Nantucket in my rearview mirror. I couldn't stand to be on this island for one more day. "This changes nothing," I said. "Once the funeral is over, there'll be nothing keeping me here. I mean, Mai is here, but she has so many people who love and support her. She'll hardly notice I'm gone."

"I doubt that. You're her special boy." Lisa was clearly relieved by my proclamation. It seemed she had been holding her breath. Now, she could exhale.

"Once I find a job in New York, I'll send her money."

"Oh, you're such a good son," Lisa said, squeezing me.

Pai's funeral wasn't the usual Cape Verdean extravaganza. Mai would have none of that. Neither she nor Pai drank and couldn't abide by all the drinking and carrying on that took place at the typical Cape Verdean funeral. They would have a simple church service. Pai would be buried in the family plot in the Catholic cemetery in the area set aside for people of color, followed by a small quiet buffet at the house for close family only.

Other than all the weeping and carrying on at the church and cemetery, the day was as Mai wished—dignified and respectful. She didn't shed a tear in public; it was almost as if she stayed strong so everyone else around her could fall apart. She hadn't yet acknowledged her true loss. Mai would have Marie and Aunt Mabel to get her through this. Fortunately, they were there for Mai that day, but the days to come would prove difficult.

So much of losing loved ones includes attending to all the details, arrangements, and managing condolences. Mai's grieving would come in time. Mai and Pai had been married forty years and had never spent a day apart, although most of his days were consumed by work and worry about work. He wasn't always home by dinner, but he was there at bedtime like clockwork, a dependable husband, unlike so many others, who were out boozing, gambling, and womanizing long past midnight. He was truly a good man.

TWENTY

....

LABOR DAY WAS ALWAYS THE FIRST MONDAY IN September, making for a long weekend. Lisa decided to leave on Sunday to beat the crowd. Lisa had a lot to do at home to prepare for my arrival.

"I'll be there by the 21st for sure, probably sooner. I can't wait to get off this island," I said. I was anxious to start my new life as a big city boy in love.

Since quitting my job at the Pleasant Inn, I had picked up some work closing up rich folks' houses. The extra cash would come in handy. I had scored the work through Aunt Mabel, of course.

The Claymoores had a huge home on Upper Main Street. They also had several cars they left on the island in the off-season. One of my many tasks was to get the cars winterized and then put up on blocks in their garage. Two of the vehicles had already been serviced. The third car was a 1940 red convertible Plymouth Roadster—a shiny beauty with huge white-walled tires. I had saved this one for last because I wanted to drive Lisa to the boat in style.

Our separation wasn't marked by anxiety or grief. We kissed, held each other, and let go easily, knowing the separation was the last goodbye before we started our life together. When we waved, she on the ferry and I on the shore, it wasn't dramatic or bittersweet.

It was merely a comma or a pause in our lives without the finality of a period or the dramatic flair of an exclamation point. But had I known what I know now, I would've watched her go until she and the boat were out of sight. When the ferry rounded Brant Point, I returned to the Roadster parked prominently across the street. I had a spring in my step, knowing that the gorgeous red convertible was mine, if only for a day.

The Claymoores had left a week earlier. They never stayed for Labor Day, not wanting to have to deal with the hordes squeezing out the last bit of summer. I decided to take the Roadster for a quick joyride before returning it to its winter quarters. I knew I probably shouldn't be doing this, but no one would know once I had it tucked away for the season.

Feeling the leather seat against my backside and the wind in my hair, I gripped the smooth steering wheel, beaming. I imagined for a minute this car was mine, and I could take it wherever I wished, even off the island and anywhere my heart desired. I could go to New York, Boston, Washington, or even drive across the expanse of the U.S. to Los Angeles or San Francisco. I checked myself out in the mirror and liked what I saw—a vibrant, confident man, even a tad handsome. Could I say, *Man*? After this summer, I believed I could.

I drove to Polpis Road, the perfect strip of road to put the Roadster through its paces. The road wasn't that long, but it had a few hills and turns to make the drive challenging and exhilarating. I wished Lisa were with me to enjoy the rush! We'd laugh, throw our heads back, and revel in the speed. The speedometer said it could do 80 mph, but I doubted it could go that fast.

Once I cleared town, I stepped on the accelerator and watched the speedometer climb to 55, 60, 65, 68, the world whizzing by in a blur. My attention was torn between the speedometer and the road. Just past the turnoff for Wauwinet, there was a sharp curve, which the car handled nicely. I glanced up after checking the speedometer to see a deer standing in the middle of the road staring at me with its huge doe eyes. As I swerved to avoid the creature, the right front tire caught the shoulder, and I lost control. I attempted to steer the Roadster back onto the road, but the vehicle skidded sideways, throwing the right rear wheel into a ditch. It flipped violently, expelling me from the driver's seat. As I flew through the air, I thought, *if this is it, at least I had this summer.* At least I had Lisa. I was thrown into the scrub brush a distance away from the vehicle. The momentum caused the vehicle to flip again, and finally it came to rest well off the road.

At first, I had no idea where I was and how I got there. My senses slowly returned. I remembered the deer, the sky, and then the blackness. I must have been knocked unconscious by the impact. I glanced at the vehicle lying on its side. Then I checked myself for wounds. I was relieved to find no blood or blood-stained clothes. My limbs appeared to be attached. A wave of anxiety that had arisen vanished.

I attempted to pull myself up, but my body was caught on something. I looked down to see if there was a tree branch or boulder on top of me. But there was nothing. I was pinned down by an invisible force pressing me against the earth. I tried to mobilize, but my legs were dead weight. The anxiety that seconds earlier was quelled, spiked, and radiated to my useless limbs—all pumped up with adrenaline but pinned like an exhausted wrestler reluctant to admit that his opponent had won. But, in this case, who was my opponent? *What is wrong with me? Why can't I move? Did I sever...?* I couldn't let my mind go there. If I did, it would be like giving up on the one life I had. The one body I had been given. I was filled with a deep sense of foreboding, like something might be terribly wrong, and there was no way to reverse the course, re-live the day for an entirely different outcome.

Then I panicked for a different reason. If I couldn't move, how could I get help? How could anyone find me? I would lie dying, and no one would know. But the fact that the car was rolled over on its side would garner attention. In a big city, residents might drive past me, but on this intimate island, people were nosey and helpful in equal parts. Someone was sure to find me.

As the light quickly faded, the dampness descended, a precur-sor to the fog that would drift in. As darkness fell, legions of mos-quitos, the size of baby birds emerged. They swarmed, biting every exposed area of my body with impunity. Later, I'd discover that my right shoulder was dislocated, and my right wrist was broken. How unfair that I had just one working arm with which to fend them off. They were biting me on that hand as I futilely waved it about. Finally sated, the mosquitos stopped feasting after many hours. By then, I was covered in welts and had just one hand for scratching the irritated skin.

In the early dawn, the mosquito brigade returned for a break-fast feast. One working arm was not enough to enable me to move in any direction without generating excruciating pain. I lay there thinking about Lisa, concerned that I wouldn't be at the phone booth to receive her call.

It wasn't until mid-day that a truck pulled up next to the rolled-over Roadster. I had nearly given up on anyone finding me. I had concluded that I would die from mosquitos feasting on me before I died of thirst and hunger. As deaths went, perishing from a swarm of tiny flying vampires sucking my blood seemed like a gruesome way to go. It was then I heard Joseph's voice shouting.

Relief overtook me, but a terror reemerged. *What is wrong with my legs?* A part of me hoped I would never find out.

"Over here! I'm over here!" I cried out.

He stood over me with panic in his eyes. This made me panic even more because as a combat veteran, he had seen it all. "What the hell happened?"

"A deer."

I didn't have to say anymore. Deer plastered on car grills were a common occurrence on the island.

He kneeled next to me. "Can you get up?"

"No, I broke my wrist." I held it up to show him.

"Can you walk if I stand you up?"

"No, my legs aren't working."

"Holy shit." He touched my leg. "Can you feel that?"

"No."

He tried the other leg.

"Nope."

"Holy shit," he said again and held his head in his hand. "Maybe there's a simple explanation. I saw that in combat—guys would be paralyzed temporarily but then would regain the use of their legs."

Paralyzed? I felt dizzy and nauseated upon hearing the word. I wanted to be like his buddies in combat. *I would be okay—right? I'd heal and be good as new.*

Joseph wasn't a big guy, but manual labor had built up his muscles, so picking me up was no problem. My legs dangled uselessly as he carried me. It was a strange sensation as if they were there but not there. Joseph placed me gingerly into the cab of his truck and rushed me to Nantucket Cottage Hospital.

The doctors reset my broken wrist, relocated my shoulder, and did exploratory surgery on my lower spine.

When I emerged from the fog of anesthesia, the surgeon stood over me with a grim expression. "I'm sorry to tell you, Mr. Monteiro, but you have lost the function of your legs."

What? How can that be? "Will I ever walk again?"

The doctor shook his head. "I'm afraid not."

I thought about never again walking the streets, strolling on the beach, running on trails, my legs carrying me on island explorations, my legs giving me the freedom to roam, the legs I had taken for granted. A thick sob caught in my throat, and I cleared my gullet to make it go away, but the anguish had taken hold.

"Do you need a minute?" he asked. "I can come back. I can also get you a priest."

"Well, I'm not dead. At least not yet."

"Yes, but a priest can also comfort the living."

I didn't need comfort. I just needed my legs back. "No, it's okay. Please continue."

The doctor explained that had I been found sooner, they may have been able to relieve the pressure on the nerves in the spinal cord, but all those hours I lay waiting to be discovered had caused those nerves to atrophy, and nerve cells do not regenerate.

"I'm afraid you'll be in a wheelchair for the rest of your life."

I lay there in my hospital bed, the tears streaming down my cheeks. My life was over.

"I'm so terribly sorry." He patted my shoulder and left, clearly feeling that the emotional effects of practicing medicine were outside his purview.

But what could he do? He was just the messenger. I cursed myself for being a careless kid, unable to weigh the risks of reckless driving, unable to foresee a future without legs to carry me to my dreams. *Why did I have to take the Roadster for a stupid, careless joyride?* I began the ride as a kid and emerged as an old man.

Mai and Marie had come by to see me. Joseph returned and brought Sarah with him. No sign of Freddie. It was just his way. He avoided life's situations for reasons only known to him.

Another day passed, and I was left alone with my thoughts spiraling out of control. The nurses and doctors monitoring me, asking me questions, giving me meds was all a blur. At first, I wondered how I could end it all. *Because if I can't walk, then life isn't worth living.* To be handicapped and pitied was a fate worse than death.

When my thoughts turned to Lisa, a shroud of darkness enveloped me that I couldn't shake no matter what I tried. One thing was for sure—it was over between us. She wouldn't want to be with a cripple, and I didn't need her pity. Seeing pity in her eyes would kill me; it would destroy any remaining shred of dignity I had. I didn't even want her to know what happened. It never crossed my mind that her love was strong enough to transcend the physical realm—that she might love my heart and my mind enough to not care about my useless legs.

I had to call Lisa and let her know I wouldn't be moving to New York. What excuse would I make up? I dialed her number at least 15 times before summoning up the courage to complete the call. When I heard Lisa's voice, my heart melted, solidified, then broke into a thousand tiny shards of hurt.

"Lisa," I stammered, "I'm not going to be able to make it to New York anytime soon. Mai isn't doing well, and she needs me." My words were unconvincing, but it was the best I could muster.

"In that case, I'll come to you," she said, resolute.

"I'm sorry, Lisa. I was lying. I just don't love you, and I don't want to live in New York."

"Danny, stop lying and tell me what's going on," she pled. "I know you love me. You can tell me." she said, sobbing.

Her crying made me feel vulnerable and broken. Tears streamed down my cheeks and into my mouth, but I wouldn't let Lisa hear me cry. Then she would know I was lying. Then she would do whatever it took to convince me to reconsider. "Listen, it was just a summer thing. You need to get over it and move on," I said, trying to prevent my voice from cracking.

"Danny, please stop saying all those terrible things! You're hurting me. Danny, I love you. Please!"

I wanted to say, *you were everything to me until I became nothing.*

Lisa was hysterical when I pushed the button on the cradle to disconnect the call. The dial tone droned on as I held the receiver in my lap. The drone was a perfect metaphor for how I felt—dead inside, dead outside. The world, once awash in color, was now black and white. No, not even that. The world was gray as far as the eye could see. Nothing would ever be the same.

I knew I would never go to her, not as Pai's words echoed within me. *What if she had some illness that required you to take care of her for the rest of your life?* I loved her too much to do that to her. My life may have been cut off at the knees, but I didn't want her to be limited by a shrunken life. My life ended before it even began.

I also didn't want her be with me in Nantucket because I feared that we would become like the other Cape Verdeans who remained on the island—like my brother and his wife Sarah, where love had turned to loathing. I knew that my life with Lisa in New York would have been my ticket out—my freedom. It would have taken time, but I would have adjusted to city life and maybe even became a famous writer, heralded for my inspired prose, powerful storytelling. I would have hosted literary salons and readings, well-attended by my fans and aspiring young writers, maybe even other highly acclaimed writers. I would have mentored novelists and memoirists alike. How easy it was to dream now that the dream was dead. What risk existed when I would never put it to the test.

Life in Nantucket for the two of us would have been a death sentence given what we had shared. I'd rather end it now and preserve the enchanted summer of '42 than see our love slowly eroded by the twin tides of prejudice-induced poverty and active repression imposed by Nantucket winters and the dominant social class. And now, to make matters worse, I dreaded the scorn toward the disabled. I dreaded being tossed aside by able-bodied people. I couldn't bear to have her see me through that lens.

"Goodbye, Lisa, my love," I whispered, long after I had pushed the button on the cradle to disconnect the call. I held the handset against my heart.

I died that Labor Day when my car veered off the road into the Moors; my life, my dreams, and my hopes shattered, destroyed, irrevocably altered. I had laid there in the Moors, unable to move much more than my thoughts. To steal away from my immediate circumstance, my mind took me on a journey over the events of the summer—meeting Lisa, the beach parties, the strolls up Main Street, our island tours in Freddie's old truck, the fairground rides, the teddy bear I "won" for her, our bluefish adventure in Madaket, our first kiss, the first time we made love, and Sonya's generosity. I relived every moment I spent with Lisa. Thoughts of her sustained me through the night, the pain, the loneliness, and the onslaught of mosquitoes. What I didn't know was that night was a sneak preview of what lay ahead—thoughts of Lisa would sustain me throughout my life; keep me going when all else was bleak. I lived for that summer. I lived knowing that magic was possible, even if it only happened once in a lifetime. Sometimes you live for the past because that's all you have. That is enough for me.

When I awoke the next morning and remembered what I had become, a shiver swept over my body—the part of it I could still feel. It came not from a chill in the air but deep from within, a biting coldness, a stark confrontation with the realization that a door had been slammed shut, locked, and the key thrown away. It wasn't a physical death. That would have been kinder. It was a spiritual death, a death of happiness, of possibility, of promise—a living death.

Pai's caution resounded within me as I lay broken in my hospital bed. "Dia di sabi e ves di fedi." Laugh today cry tomorrow.

TWENTY-ONE

....

IT PAINED ANNA TO SEE DANIEL SO DETACHED FROM the world, so disengaged from life with no purpose, no hope, nothing to look forward to, just waiting to die. Peering through Daniel's lens, Anna realized longevity could be a curse. He had shared that all his known relatives had predeceased him. But Anna couldn't accept this; she presumed Daniel must have family out there, somewhere.

She made it her mission to find someone, a next of kin, who could awaken his spirit, connect him to his past, and draw him into the future. As an experienced writer and researcher, she thought, *I can do this.*

It took her a while pouring over town records without results. Then she remembered Daniel saying his sister Marie moved to Rhode Island and Eugenia to California, Anna widened her search and checked Cape Verdean communities in New Bedford, Providence, Boston, and as far as Redding, California.

It took a lot of digging and some luck, but she found a man named Daniel Teixeira, who appeared to be Marie's grandson, Michael Jr.'s son. Daniel Teixeira was a 42-year-old entrepreneur, the owner of CourseWare, Inc., an extremely successful computer education and training company. He had contracts with all the big high-tech firms, including Apple, Microsoft, Oracle, Cisco, and he was a multimillionaire.

Anna called him, a little apprehensive at first, not sure she had the right person and less sure she was doing the right thing, but she felt drawn to the task. He was surprised and delighted, to say the least. He said that he knew little of his family's history on his father's side and virtually nothing about Nantucket.

Two weeks later, Daniel Teixeira was standing in the doorway of his great-uncle's room at Our Island Home with Anna. He was dashing, slender, and wore sleek business casual clothing, projecting class, and confidence but also an air of humility.

Daniel Monteiro was slumped in his wheelchair, staring out the window at nothing.

"Mr. Monteiro, I brought someone I'd like you to meet," Anna said, with a lilt in her voice.

Daniel, feeling like that was impossible at this stage of life, slowly straightened and engaged his wheelchair's controls. He figured it was yet another healthcare professional who was going to talk aches, pains, and disorders. Daniel didn't want to spend one more second on such inane nonsense, even if it meant he'd go undiagnosed. *So be it!*

He backed his wheelchair away from the window in slow motion and swiveled around. He stared for a few seconds at the stranger in the room with Anna. One thing was for sure. A Cape Verdean could always recognize a fellow Cape Verdean in a crowd or alone without any context; there was something indelible in their features. So, too, could Daniel Monteiro recognize family across the generations. It was almost as if he saw a ghost from his past, a past he never thought he'd revisit—not in this lifetime anyway. Without exchanging any words, his eyes brimmed with tears. The man was a composite of Marie, Michael, and Michael Junior. Could he even see himself in this handsome guy? He had to be no one other than Marie's grandson.

His words caught in his throat. "What… what's your name, son?" he asked, wiping the tears from his cheeks.

"Daniel. My father, Michael, said he named me after his favorite uncle. I guess that's you!"

Daniel never knew this about his nephew, Michael. He never thought he was anyone's favorite. Daniel, who thought he had a handle on his emotions, fogged up again and focused on seating arrangements to divert attention from his tears. "Anna, would you be so kind as to bring in a second chair, one for Daniel, so we could have a proper visit?"

"Call me Danny", said the younger man.

"Oh, of course." Said Anna as she scurried out to locate another chair.

His grandnephew stayed standing, his hands crossed in front of him.

"Please, pull that chair over here and make yourself comfortable. Or as comfortable as you can be in this godforsaken place." Daniel had so many questions for his grandnephew but didn't want to overwhelm him.

The younger man carried the chair over, placed it in front of his great-uncle, and remained standing.

"Please, have a seat."

"Oh, I'll wait until Anna returns. Ladies first," he said with a smile.

The older man was pleased to see that his grandnephew had been properly raised.

Anna rushed in with the chair, breathless. "Did I miss anything?"

Daniel, the elder, smiled. "Nope. We're just getting started."

Anna and Danny arranged their chairs in front of Daniel, and sat.

Danny told his great-uncle about growing up in Fox Point, a Cape Verdean community in Rhode Island, his college years, meeting his wife in college, and starting his own business.

"Your grandfather would be so proud. He had a great business sense, just like you," he said, referring to Michael Sr.'s efforts to start a water taxi business. He wondered if Danny knew about his grandfather's tragic ending. He figured now wasn't the time to broach the topic and hoped they'd have many more opportunities to share their family history. "And your grandmother?" he asked, wanting but not wanting to know.

"She died of breast cancer eight or nine years ago."

"Oh, I'm so sorry to hear that. But, honestly, she's lucky. There's really no reason to stick around longer than necessary. I've stayed too long at the party."

Danny chuckled at this great-uncle's gallows humor but clearly didn't know how to respond. An awkward pause stretched on a little too long. Thankfully, Anna jumped in.

"You might be interested in knowing that your great-uncle is a writer."

"Oh, really?" Danny said. "What kind of writing?"

Daniel, swatted the air. "Oh, I just tinker with words and jot down my musings. It's certainly not good enough for public consumption."

"Well, shouldn't you let others be the judge of that?" asked Danny, smiling.

"That's the problem. If my writing saw the light of day, it might scare people back into the darkness."

Anna cut in. "Not true. He has shared some with me. He's actually quite good."

Daniel Monteiro wasn't having it. "I'm no Langston Hughes. That's for sure."

"If you ever feel like sharing it, I'd love to read your work. No pressure, though."

Clearly wanting to change the subject, Daniel Monteiro said, "How did you get the last name of Teixeira?"

"When my grandmother remarried, my father took his adopted father's name."

After an hour and a half, Daniel Teixeira glanced at his phone. "Oh, I'd better get going. I've got to be back on the mainland. But I'll be back soon with my wife and daughters. I can't wait for them to meet you! You have no idea how wonderful this was for me," he said, slapping both thighs and standing.

Oh, yes, I do. But Daniel, the elder, wasn't willing to say it—to be that vulnerable, not now anyway. He reached out for a handshake.

Daniel Teixeira said, "Oh, that's far too formal. Do you mind a hug, Uncle...Daniel?"

Daniel's outstretched hand was joined by his other hand, and Danny leaned over his great uncle's wheelchair for a hug. He embraced his Uncle Daniel for a long time, reluctantly releasing him.

Anna leaned over and kissed Daniel Monteiro on the cheek, and together she and Daniel Teixeira strolled out.

The older man was left with a barrage of emotions sweeping over him now that he was alone. But felt a newfound joy in knowing that his family lived on, even though the family name was lost. It was heartwarming to know that not only had Marie's family survived. They had prevailed over poverty, prejudice, and misfortune to raise a grandson and great-grandchildren who would not suffer the indignities of his generation and the generations before. *It is a different world and a different time. My world is gone forever.*

Several days later, Anna arrived at Our Island Home. This was to be her last official visit, but she planned to stay in touch with Daniel. Although more than a generation apart, they had formed a precious bond. They were Cape Verdeans bound together by their heritage and a shared experience.

She was intercepted on her way toward Daniel's room by Monica, his favorite nurse dressed in cheery floral scrubs.

"Oh, um," she faltered. "He's…he's uh, gone. Daniel left us last night."

"Did his grandnephew come to take him home?" Anna asked beaming.

"Oh, wouldn't that have been nice? No, I'm sorry to say he passed away."

"What? Why? I mean, he wasn't even sick or anything." Anna gazed at the floor and then back up at Monica. "I didn't even get to say goodbye."

"I'm so sorry. He passed quietly during the night. When I found him this morning, he was smiling."

The light returned to Anna's eyes, imagining him in his final moments. She was deeply saddened and, at the same time, happy that she had brought him joy in his final hours, a sense of peace and fulfillment, the circle of life. Daniel wouldn't get to meet his grandnieces, but perhaps he would meet his family on the other side. At least, that was what Cape Verdeans believed.

As Anna turned to leave, reflexively making the sign of the cross, Monica called out to her. "Can you wait just a sec?"

"Sure."

Monica scurried off and returned, carrying a package. "Ms. Fortes. I found this amongst his things. It's addressed to you."

"Oh, please, call me Anna."

"Sure, Anna."

Monica handed Anna the package and waited for her to open it, watching her every move, curious what was inside.

Anna quickly unsealed the large manila envelope. Inside were a bunch of pages with a note attached. Anna read the note aloud. "'Thank you for being my inspiration. Because of our talks, I was finally able to write my novel. I'm no Langston Hughes, but maybe someone will be interested in my story. Love, Danny.'" Anna lifted the note to reveal the title page of a manuscript. *Oh, Nantucket.* She peered up at Monica, whose misty eyes mirrored hers.

"That old coot!" Monica said with a wry smile to mask her feelings.

They laughed through tears.

"I had something for him today, too," Anna said. "But now he'll never know. That is, unless he's watching us." Anna glanced skyward. She reached into her purse to pull out a photograph. She handed it to Monica.

Monica held it up, perplexed. "Who's this?"

"You don't recognize her?" Anna asked.

Monica shook her head. "Should I know her?"

"It's the girl who sat on his dresser all these years—a more recent picture. I was able to track her down through her daughter."

"Oh! Wow! Is she still living?"

"No, she passed a while ago, but her daughter shared a story with me that would have shaken Mr. Monteiro to the core." Anna felt she needed to use his surname out of respect for the dead.

She pulled out from her backpack a worn-out, faded one-eyed Teddy bear that looked like he had been through several battles and had lost the war. He was plain brown with a light brown nose, not fancy and flashy like the new-fangled bears.

Reflexively Monica took it, not knowing exactly why.

"He told me the story of how he had won a Teddy bear for Lisa in the summer of '42. Her daughter told me that as her mother lay dying in hospice, all she wanted was the bear, and she talked endlessly about a boy named Danny. She thought maybe he was an end-of-life imaginary friend until I told her what I knew."

Monica held up the Teddy bear to look at him and then hugged him. She shook her head. "He left too soon. I wish he had known." As she handed the bear back to Anna, she didn't immediately let go. For a moment, they both clung to the raggedy old Teddy.

"I'm not sure." Anna retrieved the bear, returned it to her backpack, and placed the photo in her purse.

Monica's pager rang out, *Code blue. Code blue.* "Oh, crap! This is the hardest part of my job—trying but losing our dear ones," she said, sprinting down the hallway toward the emergency.

EPILOGUE

....

Anna Fortes swigged coffee at her desk, framed by a long picture window. She knew it wasn't a good idea to drink coffee at night, but she didn't care. She was determined to write Daniel's story as best she could to honor him. Anna poured over her notes, deciding how best to tell this tale. As she organized Daniel's meandering narrative, his words from their first meeting jumped off the page. "There's not a lot worth telling."

She hoped to prove him wrong. She didn't want the man she had grown to love to be right about this. She would just let her thoughts carry her and resist controlling the narrative. For now, anyway.

Anna started typing, her fingers flying across the keyboard like a pianist performing a finale for a packed audience.

It felt like a sad truth. The Cape Verdeans on Nantucket seemed stymied by their circumstances. They had achieved no distinction by any measure. They were simply ordinary people struggling to survive under harsh conditions imposed by others.

Those who escaped, like Cory and Genie Lima, Terry Tavares, Junior Monteiro, and even Anthony Viera, Aunt Mabel's son, were able to find happiness and success in places like New Bedford,

Boston, New York, and even as far away as Redding, California, where you could order a linguisa pizza at the local pizzeria, where Cape Verdean communities thrived, where the culture and traditions remained strong through community-active associations and large numbers of like-minded people.

By contrast, those who remained in Nantucket languished, eked out a living, played by other people's rules, and shrunk themselves not to threaten the status quo. Cape Verdeans were locked in a cycle of subsistence living. The diaspora that prompted families to leave the Cape Verde Islands and seek refuge in Nantucket was repeated on a much smaller scale. Those who departed survived, and those who remained perished.

Hall and Oats's lyrics capture this so well. "The strong give up and move on, while the weak give up and stay."

Though the social oppression of Cape Verdeans living in Nantucket in the summer of '42 was not of their making, they were complicit in their demise—they were reluctantly willing. Although an oxymoron, there's no other way to put it. They were reluctant to acknowledge their contribution to the prejudice permeating the island, yet they actively participated in it. As a woman of Cape Verdean descent, it is a bitter truth to swallow.

Anna stopped typing, sipped her coffee, and peered out into the darkness, seeing nothing but her own reflection.

Out of the corner of her eye, Daniel's manila envelope beckoned, right then she knew. She slipped out the crisp white stack of paper, flipped over the title page, and began reading.

When summer breezes blow,

They bring back memories of long ago.

When days were long and filled with joy,

When life was new,

You were a boy

GLOSSARY

....

KRIOLU WORDS AND PHRASES

Abensua bo/nhos	Bless you - one person/all
Aes ta ba dodu	They go crazy
Boneka	Doll
Branku(a)	A white Person
Bufatadu na boka	A slap in the face (idiom)
Buru, ka teni nau…	Stupid, you don't have…
Cachupa	Corn and bean stew
Canja	Chicken soup
Cretcheu	Sweetheart
Da en benson	Give me your blessing
Desculpam	Forgive me
Dia di sabi e ves di fedi	Laugh today, cry tomorrow (idiom)
Dios ba ku bo/nhos	God go with you - one person/all
Dios fika ku bo	God stay with you
E bo ki sabe You know/best – sarcasm meaning you don't know what you're talking about	
E ka ninhun dia nem tenpu	This is neither the time or place
El e bo familha	He's your family

Fika kaladu	Remain silent
Grogue	Alcohol or national drink of Cape Verde
Jagacida	Rice and beans
Jaime	James
Jose	Joseph
Kantu tristi	How sad
Kriolu	Cape Verdean Language or Cape Verdean Person
Kuidadu	Careful – as an admonition
Linguisa	Pork sausage
Mai	Mother or mom
Manchupa	Pork Stew
Melada	Dirty
Merkanus di kor	Americans of color – u masculine, a feminine
Mininus	Children
Mutu obrigadu	Thank you
N ka ta konprende	I don't understand
N sta un bedjisa	I'm an old fogie (idiom)
N ta papia pedra bo ta kudi pou	I'm speaking paper you're answering stick – meaning – you're not listening
Nha	My
Nha Terra Longe	My faraway land
Nhami-babu	Sweet potato picker (idiom)
Pai	Father or dad
Papai	Grandfather
Pastel d'atum	Fried dough, tuna, onion, and spices
Pudim de leite	Flan
Se so Dios ki sabe	Only God knows
Si N podi da bo un konsedju	If I can give you some advice

Sodade ta matam	The longing is killing me
Sufri kaladu	Suffer in silence
Toma un xikra di café/xa	Have a cup of coffee/tea
Xinta	Sit
Xinta, nha fidja	Sit my child

PRONUNCIATION KEY

A	*Is pronounced like **a**re*
AI	*Is pronounced like h**ig**h*
E	*Is pronounced **ei**ght*
I	*Is pronounced **e**asy*
J	*Is pronounced like the last syllable in plea**sure***
Jaime	*Is pronounced with the J sound plus D**ime***
Nh	*Is pronounced like o**ni**on*
O	*Is pronounced like the o in sore*
Tx	*Is pronounced like **chi**ef*
U	*Is pronounced like the o in s**oo**n*
X	*Is pronounced like fi**sh** or **s**it*

Disclaimer – My knowledge of kriolu is experiential not academic. There are spelling variations with pronouns and articles, variations with nouns and many other nuances with verbs and tenses. But give it a shot. **Dios ba ku bo.*

Made in the USA
Middletown, DE
04 October 2021

49585981R00154